HOLLAN L. MCCARTHY

DEDICATION

For Eric and Jeanette
because all we have to do is talk
and magic happens.
&
For my Mom and Dad
who raised all their children
in the heart of a forest.

CONTENTS

PROLOGUE

The turtle's flat shell was crisscrossed in a hexagonal pattern. His reptilian head was unevenly rounded, while his beaky mouth curved downward in a sharp point. Despite the hostile expression, his heavy-lidded eyes were dew bright. Occasionally, he blinked one of them.

He sat half-hidden under a rotten log, on the mossy banks of a stream. Around him, early morning mist drifted in the air, leaving a faint glimmer on leaves. The stream splashed along noisily. It hummed in the turtle's head, soothing his long wait. For several hours now, the bubble of water had been the only sound in the silent forest.

A ray of light slanted through the mist, falling on the turtle where he sat. Faint gleams of gold shone along the deeper lines on his back, as if he had been marked there with a fine-tipped paintbrush.

Through the sound of flowing water came another sound. Heavy footsteps shook the ground. Still not moving, the creature turned one eye slightly, and glanced toward a thick clump of trees.

Out of the trees stepped a giant man. His dark blue cloak was held close about his sizable frame. As he moved into sight, the hood of his cloak didn't hide his large nose or the flash of gold in his ears.

Spotting the turtle, he crossed the clearing and sank to the ground near the creature with surprising grace. He folded his feet underneath him. When he spoke his voice was deep, rich, and musical.

"I'm sorry I took so long," he said in an apologetic tone.

The turtle blinked but said nothing. He moved a bit to the left and slapped both tail and clawed foot on the ground impatiently.

The man threw back his hood, revealing a dark-skinned, weather-beaten face. His black and silver hair was short and thick.

"I stayed until it wasn't safe to be there, which is why I'm so late." He gave the turtle's shell a poke. "I'm glad to find you here. Have you been waiting long?"

The turtle didn't answer. The giant man's words filled him with a sinking sensation, and it took some getting used to. He shuffled and gave the trees around them a grouchy, appraising look.

The large man, unperturbed by the creature's prolonged silence, took out a soft leather pouch and shook some dried tobacco into his wide palm. Removing an intricately carved wooden pipe, he filled it slowly. When he was finished, he snapped his fingers and the tobacco began to burn on its own. A foggy, blue smoke rolled over the edge of the pipe and trickled down the stem.

"Malius has overthrown Stoneham and the King and Queen have fled," he sighed between puffs.

The turtle looked grieved, closing his eyes.

Castle Stoneham lay several miles outside the boundaries of the forest. It sat on a wide plain, a backdrop of mountains cradling behind it. Its lofty warm stone towers and arches flung a dignified presence into the golden air and awed visitors with its graceful design.

The turtle finally spoke, "I had hoped it would not –"

He didn't finish, but the man called Broon appeared to understand. He smoked in silence for a moment before shrugging, "It was foreseen."

He said this last kindly, offering some comfort to the creature, but the turtle was visibly shaken. This turn of events meant serious upheaval and disruption in Thornwold.

"Where have they fled?"

"They are on their way to the caverns. They should be there by now. Even now, many of their loyal servants are abandoning the castle and grounds. It was foreseen."

He repeated this last insistently, reminding the turtle of a previous conversation, but the turtle ignored him, saying bitterly, "You'd think you were on Malius's side."

"No, Ironsides, not on Malius's side," the large man explained patiently, "But in the position of holding the delicate balance of magic and fate. As we discussed, we must not interfere with Malius if things are to turn out as we hope."

"If you believe it," snorted Ironsides,

"I do," said Broon with resolution. "Anyway, it has ended conveniently enough for the new ruler of Thornwold."

The turtle made a stifled sound. "It is my opinion had the King not been so trusting, this could have been decently averted. Now we have no choice but to manage it as well as we can."

Broon frowned but was lost in thought.

"We can't fight? Is it too late? The King could rally an army and we could —"

Ironsides trailed off at the expression on Broon's face.

"There would be no use. It was not foretold we should have anything to do with the restoration of the King of Thornwold. Not yet anyway."

He puffed more blue smoke, blowing it high above the stream, where it floated in small round clouds.

Ironsides coughed pointedly. He was not fond of pipe smoke.

"The problem is Althea," said Broon, then paused.

It was too bad. He hadn't known this part was coming, but because of this unanticipated twist, he was set to the floundering task of interfering.

Ironsides again closed his eyes, his down-turned mouth sinking deeper into his wrinkled face. "Don't tell me anymore. I can't bear it."

"She is all right for now," Broon assured his old friend hastily. "It's her magic."

"What about it?" the turtle demanded. "What's it got to do with anything? All the royal family have visible magic. Which brings me to ask, why didn't they use it to defeat Malius?"

"Because Malius was cleverer than they are," admitted Broon, "Malius has stolen the Globe. What happened, you see, he —"

Ironsides was pale. Even for a turtle.

"How did he get ahold of it?" he interrupted faintly. "I had warned the King to be careful. He assured me it was too well guarded."

The glass Globe was the royal family's most treasured possession. It dated back centuries, preserving their line, and

3

protecting their legacy. Most of all, it bequeathed each new Stoneham family member with the ability to see magic, and therefore control it. To become skilled at magic, ordinary people had to take the route of learning to use something one couldn't see, but the royal family of Stoneham could see the trails of magic bursting through the air. Since the ability to see magic was something most people would cheerfully kill for, and the Globe was the most powerful magical object in that land, it was a great secret. No one outside the family, except Broon and a few others, knew anything about the Globe.

"We aren't sure yet –" said the giant, but the turtle was going from pale to bright green.

"Damn it, Broon! This watch and wait and fated attitude has bungled this from start to finish. I'm off to find the King myself!"

He began stalking away towards the stream, but Broon picked him up by the shell. "Now hold on, Ironsides!"

The turtle choked with indignation and waved his short legs helplessly. "Put me down! I will not be – handled!"

He glared and tried unsuccessfully to snap at the rough fingers just out of reach of his short neck.

Broon said nothing, but sat still, holding his hand high and watching the turtle's furious attempts to bite him with an expression of compassionate amusement.

The turtle had known this was coming. The fall of Stoneham, and the triumph of Malius. The original agreement to rescue the royal family, but to let fate run its course and do nothing. The shock of it had sent his old friend in the direction humans so often go, running off to fix, to repair, to resolve.

Broon regretted the mortal creatures. Their constant mistakes and interfering when they shouldn't. Letting the wrong things happen needlessly. He was not unsympathetic, but his immortality and the centuries it spanned left him with a deep knowledge of the world moving as it should, always on a path. If it swayed from the path, things went awry. They went awry anyway, but more so if humans took a hand.

"Always this hurry. That's the trouble with mortals; always a need to arrange and make everything as they would have it. They don't live long enough."

Broon trembled and the trees around him dimmed through a

shadow, as if a gauzy curtain had been dropped before his eyes. He shrugged the vision away. Visions were troublesome, and not always true or specific.

Broon's wildness hung off him in strands and left a strong trace where he walked. He was as connected to the forest around him as deeply as he was connected to his own heart. Without him, the forest would not be.

Century after century, he remained a figure of great importance to the ruling King or Queen of Thornwold. His presence in Stoneham this particular day was a necessity, in view of the circumstances, but the experience had left him weary.

The stolen Globe and the fall of Stoneham was poisoned smoke. Here in his forest, he was finally able to clear some of it away. The strength of his trees was filling him with everything from the air to the roots of the earth, welcoming him home.

Broon was still holding the struggling Ironsides in the air. He grinned, revealing white teeth set in his dark face.

At this insulting facial expression, the turtle's hot fury turned icy cold, and he huffily withdrew into his shell.

Broon's smile vanished and he managed to appear solemn.

"Now, now," he said to the shell in a soothing tone, "Don't be hasty, Iron. I am sorry. Here, let me put you down." He did so, depositing the turtle gently on a bed of soft moss. "Let me explain before you run off. Come on out."

He waited to see if the creature's head would appear. When it did not, he sat back with a sigh, nestling into the rough bark of the fallen log as if it were a comfortable chair.

"We are not entirely without a plan."

The opening in the shell remained silent and dark but appeared to be listening.

"We had to get the King and Queen and little Althea away quickly, of course. The instant Malius took control of the Globe it was utter chaos. The royal family were in the lower dungeons awaiting execution. We arrived just in time."

Broon took the pipe stem from his mouth and used it to poke the shell so it moved slightly. "But it's the baby Princess that has me concerned."

"Why?" said Ironsides, his head emerging. "What's happened to her?"

"Nothing, she's fine. That's what I mean. Her parents are not doing so well. It's difficult to get used to seeing the world without magic. Harder still to be unexpectedly stripped of the power of magic. They are children fumbling in the dark. It's astounding Ember and I were able to get them away. But Althea is fine. Her ability to see magic is still intact."

The turtle stared. "That's not possible."

"But it is. The possessor of the Globe, now Malius, stole the magic from the King and Queen, but he didn't take Althea's. Or perhaps he couldn't. Either way, why? It is deeply troubling."

Ironsides was alarmed but tried not to show it. "I don't like it," he said finally, nibbling a blade of grass. "Who's with them now? Ember?"

"Dominus is watching over them," said Broon casually.

"Dominus!" said the turtle in disbelief. "I don't trust him."

"I know you don't," Broon sighed, "but he is trustworthy nevertheless." He smiled slyly at the turtle. "You just don't like snakes."

"I have good reason for it," said Ironsides. "Not only that, but he was Malius's bedfellow for far too long."

"He was. Dominus has never mentioned how he got the scars on his back, but they were not put there by accident. I believe in Dominus's loyalty."

"Very well but keep him away from me." Ironsides bit a tuff of grass and chewed it absently.

"I suppose they are safe enough for now. In the caverns. What about you? What are the long-term plans?"

Broon shrugged, avoiding the question. "I have some business of my own to attend to first. Concerning Jack."

"What business?" asked the turtle curiously. "What's Jack to do with this?"

"More than you'd guess, old friend."

"I suppose you'll tell me in time. But mind you, Broon, he's a dangerous commodity, that boy."

"Precisely why we must make sure he is on our side."

"He's a child," said the turtle dismissively. "His loyalty will lie with whoever is kind to him, I suppose, but make sure you watch him for any, uh, unusual tendencies, won't you?"

"I'll see to it. I believe he will turn out to be useful. Even you must admit, Iron, he's already an unusual boy."

The turtle stretched his head and yawned sleepily, clearly bored with the subject of Jack. "What is the plan for the family?"

The giant was uncomfortable.

The turtle noted it immediately. "Broon?"

Broon hesitated, taking a long drag from his pipe.

Ironsides stared at him. "The family can stay in the caverns, can't they? Or perhaps in Lilywell?'

"Not Lilywell," said Broon, preparing for another argument. "They'll stay where they are to regain their strength. Until they can be moved."

The creature was suspicious. "Moved where?"

"To the village," said Broon, not meeting the turtle's eye.

"*Brell?*" Ironside's voice was furious and Broon looked around for escape.

"You know we don't associate with Brell folk! You know what the place is like, and why. I can't believe you would even consider – consider –"

The turtle coughed in fury. "The royal family cannot go to Brell," he finished, saying this last as if it were the final word on the subject.

Broon was even more uncomfortable. He puffed on his pipe and blew smoke into the air, while an angry silence fell. Several tense minutes passed.

"I understand, Ironsides," he finally said, his voice gentle, "but they cannot stay here."

Ironsides said nothing. He turned his back on the giant but didn't move towards the water.

Broon watched him carefully. He knocked his pipe against a nearby rock, scattering ashes and sparks. Again, he regretted the visions that escape mortal men – and creatures. He put out a large finger, tracing the golden lines on the turtle's shell. Iron stiffened but didn't move.

"The visions are vague, it's true, but I believe the answer to them lies in keeping any living heir of Thornwold as safe from harm as we can make them. Malius will not look in Brell, Iron. In fact, I am not sure he knows of it. What would you have them do? Stay in the caverns until Malius's men close in like a pack of wolves? For they will. I have seen it. Would you have me put a sleep on them, until the hero can awaken them? There is no hero in this story, Ironsides. Our only choice is to send them into the dark of Brell and cover their tracks. It is the only way I see some glimmer of hope at the end. The question remaining concerns you. Will you go too?"

The turtle can't remember when the name Brell hadn't been an evil name among the people of Thornwold. Brell lay on the borders of the Thorn, where the strangest creatures of the forest live. Only Broon went near the borders of Brell because no one else dared. The strangeness coiling around the village was as solid and smooth as an impenetrable wall of glass.

Ironsides heaved a sigh and turned back towards his friend. His eyes were suspiciously bright.

"Must it be Brell? The place is cursed, Broon."

"It may be, as you say, cursed, but Brell isn't so bad, once you get past the, er, surrounding wood. It is still a part of this country, whether it knows it or not. You will go with them?"

"Of course, I will. I am of the royal family. It is my duty to go where they go. Even into exile. Even into a cursed, miserable, evil unearthly –"

"That's the spirit, old friend!" Broon interrupted. "Now you'd better be off to the caverns to help prepare them."

"When will you be along?"

"I'll be along after I've seen to my other business." He paused, holding open his pocket teasingly. "Unless you'd care to come with me?"

"As if I would!" the turtle muttered loudly, moving toward the rushing water. "I'll see you underground," he called and dropped into the stream, disappearing with a plop.

Broon watched the place where the turtle vanished. He put away his pipe and tobacco pouch and drew his hood up over his dark face.

He gazed around him at the sunny glade. The grass was bright green and the air was clear with early sunshine. A bee was buzzing lazily in a clump of purple clover. The smell of ripening blackberry bushes drifted in the air.

"I am sorry, brothers," he said, addressing his surroundings. "But perhaps it won't be for long."

Low in his throat he made a rough humming noise, a song, but with no true melody. The sunlight in the glade darkened. A cold mist was rising out of the trees around them. The bee's buzzing stopped. He flew away shooting upward through the tangle of branches as they wove together, blocking out the morning sun. Clovers folded up green leaves, hiding their purple faces from the vanishing light. Thorns on the blackberry bushes lengthened and gleamed wickedly.

As Broon moved out of the glade, the stream still bubbled brightly. "Water," he reflected. "It will come through, no matter what."

He went deeper into the forest and the humming disappeared with him. Behind him, the trees stood silent and still in their unexpected, early autumn.

Once Upon a Time in Brell

I see the world in colors, but I cannot paint it. I only see.

I thought everyone could see colors radiating from people as I do, but Mama says no, it is something I get from she and Papa, and I shouldn't talk about it. I have never told a soul, but I can't help seeing.

Gold is love, blue is sorrow, dull green is pain, and yellow is being happy or being afraid. Anger comes out in different shades of red, but always there is a mix of colors glowing from people, and some of them I can't name. Mama explains the reason for this is because people have complicated feelings, and I will understand why as I get older.

I am only seven, but I am formally named Althea Luna Elizabeth Cecilia Morgan. It's a lot of names for a small girl, and I am never called anything except 'Thea'. I asked Mama why I had so many names, and she told me I was christened for my two grandmothers, herself, and myself.

Althea means, 'to heal'. My Papa says he picked it out himself because healing the broken bits of things is the best thing one can do in life.

Grown-ups often say mysterious things.

If you haven't been to Brell, you aren't alone, because Brell doesn't officially exist on any map. The authorities in the capital city of Moor can't decide where the boundaries are or whether Brell lies inside or outside their borders, so the village stays a betwixt-and-between place.

It always has mist around it, rising from its rivers. Especially at night. Sometimes it even fades into the mists, or so travelers have said, when they try and find it and can't.

Living in a village that doesn't officially exist can make you feel as if you don't exist. But Papa says Brell people grow up, get married, have babies, laugh, cry, eat good meals, farm their fields, sell their wares, and when they die they are buried in the cemetery near the church. He says that is as real as it gets.

The forest around Brell is old and dark. Many Brell folk refuse to set foot in it. The shallow edges of the trees and scraps of undergrowth are enough to provide wood for their fires. I think they don't go inside because of the darting shadows of small, unidentifiable things.

Maggie at the Owl's Roost laughs and says they are just small woodland creatures, but Mama says they are the guardians of the wood and steal copper coins, and food from the larder, or sometimes naughty children.

I don't think I am very naughty, so I went once and stood inside the trees. The whole place had a cold, clear smell, like water inside a cave. I had the sense I was being watched but couldn't say by whom or what. I thought I saw a pair of glowing, yellow eyes.

Papa found out and was angry. He told me I should not ever go into the forest again because I could be easily lost. I wasn't lost the first time though. I stayed in the same spot all the time and could see our house from where I stood. When I am older, I will go in and find out what all the fuss is about.

Brell lies between two deep rivers. The rivers run along a wide, dusty road and all three lead to Moor, the enormous capital city of our country.

Papa says from Moor's port, white-sailed, slow-moving ships set out for distant lands in distant seas and some of them never return.

I like the way he says this. It sets me dreaming of those ships, sailing far away. I long to see a ship. Abigail says they are like Thomas the Riverman's boat, only larger, with white sheets hung from large poles where the wind can rest to blow them over the seas. I tried to imagine this but could not.

Thomas has been to Moor. He brings his barge-boat up the river once a month, full of supplies for families and shopkeepers. I like Thomas. He was born in Brell but did not want to farm or keep a shop, so he left for Moor when he was a young man. He has built up his riverboat business, and since he is the only riverman who will travel back and forth between Brell and Moor, he makes a good living.

Thomas is large and jolly and lifts me up with strong arms to swing me round. He has a sunburned face, and his arms are covered in pretty blue and green drawings that won't wash off. I made him promise me he will draw some on my arms when I grow up, and he laughed loud and said these drawings weren't for ladies. But I am not a lady, just a village girl from Brell, so maybe it doesn't matter.

Thomas gives me oranges and sweet candy and tells me what a beauty I am growing into, like my mother. Mama smiles at this and says she wishes he would stay to supper, but he always hems and haws and says he has his 'eatables waiting for him elsewhere.' I asked Papa what are 'eatables' and he said it is only Thomas's delightful way of speaking.

Thomas's eatables are usually waiting for him at the Owl's Roost and are kept hot for him by Maggie. Maggie is large and comfortable, with soft brown hair. She laughs a good deal when Thomas comes. She puts her arms round him and hugs him tight. Thomas only stays a week in Brell, delivering and selling his wares and gathering orders from the villagers.

Maggie does not laugh when he leaves. She slams down her customer's drinks with force, and says she wishes Thomas's boat would not take a month to get from place to place, and if the whole ugly thing sank, she would be glad of it.

Bol says he and Maggie met Thomas in Moor, where they worked at an inn near the port. When Bol and Maggie moved to Brell and opened Owl's Roost, Maggie hoped Thomas would marry her, but he hasn't yet.

Bol is lovely. He is as large and comfortable as his sister, but not so laughing. Instead he has a gentle chuckle and kind eyes. He listens more than he talks, and people tell him their troubles. Bol never tells anyone his troubles, though Papa says he has the distinction of being an outsider, and that is trouble enough.

I don't know what he means, but Mama sighed when I asked her and said we are outsiders as well.

Papa says we used to live in a large city far away. He enjoys going to Owl's Roost on long winter evenings to talk with Bol about Moor. They talk about fine houses and the theatres where people dance and sing and tell stories.

I can tell both Papa and Mama miss this kind of life, though they never say so. Abigail says they will not go back, no matter how much Papa might talk to Bol, and I shouldn't worry over it.

Abigail is my parent's oldest friend, but she isn't big. She is little, only a foot taller than me, and I am small for my age. Abigail is a potions-maker and healer. Her kitchen is full of strange herbs and bottles that sparkle on their own.

I am never allowed to touch any of these, but once I laid a finger on a bottle of coppery stuff when no one was looking, and it hummed at me cheerfully.

My eyes are a different shape and color than other people's eyes. They are a shade of blue I can't describe, and too large with slightly oval centers instead of round. The rims of them are gold. I suppose it is why I see colors. Maggie says I have 'cat's eyes' and Papa smiles and says my eyes are pools of blue and gold, so I see the world with equal parts love and sadness.

Owl's Roost is a large inn, with dark, smoke-stained beams. The shelves hold lots of different bottles of ale, and there is an uneven stone fireplace where warm fires blaze in winter. Not many Brell villagers have been to Moor, but travelers from other places sometimes come dripping and weary through the mist and the dark. They are glad to find warmth and rest at Owl's Roost.

In the storeroom, near the back entrance of the inn, is a ladder leading to a space between the chimney and the sharp slant of the roof. Climbing up it, you'll find a small, open attic where Maggie stores extra ale and hangs herbs and boxes of spices from nails driven into the wall. It is strangely cool there in summer, and cozy in the winter.

I often sneak into it while no one is watching, slipping in through the back entrance and into the storeroom, which is never locked, and scurrying up the ladder. Below this attic is an opening looking down into the common room below. If I sit near the edge of this, I can hear the people talking without being seen.

Bol knows I do it because he caught me one evening, slipping down the ladder. He only laughed and gave my bottom a slap and ordered me to go home. I am more careful now not to be seen. Maggie would tell my Mama, but only because she thinks I am too young for some of the talk she calls 'bawdy'.

Hiding here is where I first learned the old story about Brell and how it is rumored to be cursed. Travelers around the fire tell each other that someday this village will disappear into the mists forever. They say it is because of an ancient bargain made with the river spirits, and the clock is ticking away toward the end. I'm not sure I want to know if I live in a cursed village.

Villagers say it is all nonsense, but everyone in Brell is plagued by the uncanny silence of the trees and the persistent, heavy sound of the mist drip, drip, dripping from leaves. It sometimes wakes me up. I asked Mama about this, but she told me I was only dreaming, and not to be afraid, because I am safe as long as I have she and Papa and Ironsides.

Ironsides is my turtle. Mama gave him to me when I was only four, admonishing me to take good care of him. I keep him in my pocket, when I am not balancing him on my shoulder, where he grips with his claws.

He is a very smart turtle, and often blinks his eyes at me in a way that makes me think he understands what I am saying perfectly well, but being a turtle, can't tell me so. Mama says he has been with our family a long time, even before I was born. I asked Papa how old he was, but he said he didn't know exactly.

Ironsides has faint golden lines on his back, but I can't tell if they are painted on or part of him. He comes with me everywhere I go, and sleeps on my pillow at night, cuddled against my head.

Mama died when I was ten, from a fever that made her too weak to stand or walk. Her breath would often leave her and when she coughed, she coughed blood. Abigail gathered herbs to cure her, but none of the mixtures she made helped.

She died in the night, holding my hand to one side of her face and Papa's hand on the other side. I couldn't cry, but Papa wept. The color exploded out of them both and melted into the loveliest shade of blue and green and gold. The colors dimmed until they only hovered round Papa and I, and Mama's life faded and left her. Papa's colors turned into a swirling shade of sea-green sadness, but I did not produce any color.

I didn't know if this was because one can't see their own emotions, or because I was so numb. Mama was gone and there was no one to ask. I held Ironsides tightly that night, and it wasn't until Papa came in and gathered me up in his arms, I was able to cry.

Wrapped as our house was in grief, it took a little time for me to notice Papa was changing. He often paused during everyday talk and forgot what he was saying. He stopped looking at me. He would stand at the window for hours, gazing across the river and into the forest. He thought he saw Mama in the trees.

She is there, he would say, *waiting for me*.

I would sooth him and tell him he must be dreaming, noting how his eyes didn't see me. I worried, but told no one, convincing myself he would soon be all right again. I was a fool.

One evening, he rested his hand on my head and said he was going out. I clung to him, fearful.

"Where, Papa," I asked, but he turned roughly away.

"Your Mama is waiting for me," he said.

I leaped to my feet to stop him, but I was small, and he shoved me aside.

"It's all right, Thea," he said, but his eyes shone oddly.

He went out our front door and gate, picking his way down the steep bank to the shallow part of the river. He waded across and climbed up into the fringes of the forest trees.

I stood in the doorway, trying not to cry, trying to hope and believe he would look for my Mama, and when he did not find her he would come to his senses, realizing he had been acting as a man in a dream.

He turned once, giving me a re-assuring wave. The November stars grew brighter as he went deep into the woods. The black trees swallowed him up. Far away on the steps of our small house, my eyes wide and burning from lack of sleep, I waited shivering until dawn, but Papa did not come back.

He never came back.

People said sorrowfully he must have been lost and killed by wild animals, his mind unhinged by my Mama's death, but I could not believe it. After this, I would dream about him, and always he was turning away from me at the edge of black trees.

Our house was sold at auction. I went to live with Abigail in her cottage built from river stone, near the road leading to the outside world.

In the river below her house, there are worn step-stones, each lying within a few feet of the other, crossing the shallow water to an island of rock and sand. On the other side of the small island, the water is deep and cold. Beyond this is the forest.

I like to step out onto the stones and sit in the middle of the rushing water, hearing nothing but the bubble of the current. The island lying safely between me and the threatening trees.

I was farther from Owl's Roost here, and missed Maggie and Bol, but I would run into the village to see them whenever I could.

I continued to see Thomas every month. He would always stop his barge on the island, leaping with agility across the rocks to leave me sweet candy and oranges, as well as different boxes of ingredients for Abigail's potions.

The first time he saw me, after Mama had died and Papa had

gone, he hugged me tightly and blew his nose on a large, red handkerchief. I wanted to make him happy, so I said I wished he would stay for supper, but it only made him blow his nose again. Murmuring something about 'eatables', he took himself off upriver to Maggie.

Abigail was kind. She did everything a parent should do for a child. She made me sit up straight, go to bed early, and eat cooked vegetables, which I detested.

As ordinary as my childhood might be, I began to perceive the differences between Abigail and I and the residents of Brell.

In my small world of Mama and Papa and Owl's Roost, I had not noticed any particular dislike, but now the rejection was clear. The villagers might speak politely to me and to Abigail, but their eyes were cold. The color of dislike and distrust is a grayish orange, melting into some color one can't see, like a shadow at the corner of your eye.

This didn't stop them from buying her potions when they could, and trading for them when they couldn't. Abigail's potions stemmed your fever, helped you find wood for your fire, healed wounds and kept the wild animals away from your henhouse.

The people of Brell did not approve of Abigail, but they clamored for her cures. When a family member was ill, it was Abigail who was summoned to use her healing skills.

"I advise you to get an education, Thea," Abigail said one soft evening. "Learn to read, and write, and figure simple mathematics." She drew a deep breath and her old eyes gazed at me wistfully. "I've never had children. Perhaps you will promise me that someday you will train as my apprentice."

I did not much like the idea of going to school, but learning potion-making someday sounded fine, so I promised her carelessly enough. I didn't know how the promise would change everything.

On my first day of school, the other children whispered to one another. Abigail was a witch and I was her witch-daughter. I was ten and understood Abigail was a healer. I did not know what a 'witch' was or why it was a bad thing to be. When I said this, the other children laughed, but would not answer.

I ran to Owl's Roost after school, and was soothed by Maggie, who fussed over me and railed against the silly children who had made me cry. The slices of cake she gave me sweetened my hurt feelings, but I knew I must not be a baby. I did not want Abigail to know.

"I must put up with it, Maggie," I said.

Maggie understood, but I could see the love and longing seeping out of her, like an azure and gold summer evening.

Despite the bullying, I was good at lessons, especially reading. Master Patterson, the teacher, liked me well enough to lend me books, and soon I was reading not only fairy tales, but grown-up books: philosophy, history, science, books about music and art and geography. I devoured them all.

I was quick with answers to questions and did well on exams. Being smart did not make me popular, but having no friends left me plenty of time for studying.

The abuse I experienced at school grew from sneers to insults to the occasional 'accidental' assault with stones or sticks. I bore it in silence. My instincts told me children fought their own battles and so I did not complain. The bruises, I explained to Abigail and Maggie and Bol, came from rough games during play. My solitary walks home I excused on the grounds that Abigail's cottage was out of the way. The adults watched me with sympathetic eyes, but to my relief, they did not say much.

The worst of it went on for the first two years, until one day came the accusation that my Papa had left me because I was small and odd. They said he hadn't loved me.

In front of my eyes rose the image of Papa, waves of gold rising from him when he looked at Mama and me. The memory of his shoulders slumped, broken by grief, as he walked away from me into the dark mass of trees.

Without thinking, I picked up a heavy stick of firewood from the schoolhouse porch and stepped forward, striking the speaker. The bully held his bloody face and wept and ran, but the other children, their eyes wide, backed away from me in fear.

Vanishing around me in traces of black smoke, was the color of vengeance. It was the first time I had seen myself produce color. It was bright red shot with silver veins. It frightened me. But after this, the 'accidents' stopped.

I went to school until two years ago. I was fourteen and had had to lengthen my hem and catch my hair back with pins. I came home one day and told Abigail there was nothing more to be learned at the village school. I wiped my sweaty palms on my skirt.

In Moor was a famous university. It taught both men and women. With the encouragement of my teacher, I had begun to study for the difficult entrance exams. I loved Abigail, but all my reading and studies had taught me to long for a wider world.

Fidgeting, I explained this to Abigail. I was nearly fifteen, I said. Nearly grown up. I was never going to fit in here. Master Patterson thought I was clever enough to pass the exams. I could study teaching or philosophy or science.

Abigail's face was hard and grieved. Stiffly, she reminded me I had promised to be her apprentice. I smiled at first, thinking she could not mean it.

I still had not one single friend my age. My fellow villagers eyed me with suspicion and distrust. There was no future for me here.

Abigail only set her jaw and shook her head. I was bound to her, she insisted angrily. Bound by the promise I had made her at the age of ten.

My smile faded as I realized she was serious. My first instinct was to argue, but the words died in my throat. Abigail had taken me in. She had loved me. She had raised me. I could not go back on my word to her, even if it weren't fair. I turned away from her and fought back tears of disappointment.

"I need to pass on my knowledge," Abigail said to my back. She was kind enough to sound regretful. And that was that.

I stayed home and became her official apprentice.

Thomas married Maggie. I helped out Maggie and Bol in the inn during the summer because the warmer months meant more travelers passing through Brell on the dry roads. Bol paid me a good wage, and I was carrying a load of empty glasses into the kitchen to be washed when Thomas came in through the door.

"Maggie, my girl," he said, and I looked up, startled, since it was the first time Thomas had ever shown up in Brell twice in one month.

It was the middle of summer when the air is hot and breathless, and everything feels sticky. Thomas hung up his hat on a peg in the entryway of the inn while Maggie stared at him before bursting into noisy tears.

Thomas hastened to take her in his arms. "There, there," he murmured as he stroked her hair. "There, there."

I fled the room, not wanting to spy on such a private moment and found Bol outside near the woodshed. I blurted out that Thomas had come to marry Maggie at last. When we went back inside, Maggie was smiling and sitting on Thomas's knee.

"There will be a wedding before the month is out," Maggie said. "I've waited long enough for it."

Thomas was content. "I'm tired of being a Riverman. No more long trips for me."

His young cousin was going to take over his barge and business, so it was all right, but I would miss Thomas bringing me sweets and oranges and said so. At this, he picked me up and swung me round like I was a little girl again, proving he was still the strongest man on the river.

"I'll be just down the road now," he said, "and you can run in and see me whenever you have a mind to."

So we were all happy and Bol got out some special wine to toast the couple's future.

I was the bridesmaid at the wedding, wearing a new dress of pale blue. Several of the young men bothered me for a dance. I don't know how to dance, so I declined. Most of them were the boys who had said mean things to me in school. Walking away home, Abigail gave me a hopeful look.

"Perhaps they have come to like you, Thea. Children change as they get older. You are striking, as your mother was."

I snorted at this. She was smiling at the road ahead, dreaming I would marry and have children she could call her grandchildren. I kicked a loose stone in the path. No boy my age in Brell had ever been kind to me.

When I got home, I went to the attic where I sleep and looked in my glass. At Owl's Roost, strangers sometimes stared at me and not because I was pretty. My nose was long and thin. My mouth too wide. I had the unlucky feature of having ears slightly uneven and too large for my head. I was small for my age and too thin.

But my heavy red hair gleamed darkly, as Mama's used to, and my eyes were unusual. Abigail said they shimmer with their own faint golden light. I didn't look like any of the villagers from Brell, who tend to be tall, fair, and sturdily handsome.

But interesting eyes or not, I was ordinary, except for the special gift of seeing colors, which I had never told anyone about, not even Abigail.

Lately, I have other secrets. I have bad dreams I can't remember, and when I wake up there are strange sounds near my window. Odd flying shadows, black against the night swoop from the trees. They thump the cottage and zoom back into the branches, quick as frogs jumping into a pool.

Once I thought I heard someone calling my name. I couldn't help but think about my Papa, undone by grief, hearing Mama calling to him. I worry about the state of my mind.

Since leaving school I haven't felt like myself. I feel numb and far away. Sounds mute and people's voices recede. I forget to pay attention to what is happening around me.

I don't want to worry Abigail, or Bol, or Maggie and Thomas, so I whisper the secrets to Ironsides. My old turtle is still living with no sign of aging. I tell him how I long to break my promise to Abigail and run away from Brell and attend the university in Moor. How I wish I had the courage. I tell him about the things worrying me and about the dark thumping things at the window. He listens, perking up his head and blinking his eyes at me in what I think is a sympathetic way.

The Stranger

"Magic," muses Abigail, "has many uses. It can be dangerous. It can be hard to master. It takes many years of commitment and study to learn, and it takes many years of practice to fully understand how and where to use it. Magic can corrupt the good, and it can heal evil. It is both dark and light."

I nod, because it is easier to agree than to ask for a further explanation of something that confuses me already. I push a stray hair from my eyes. I bind up a bundle of dandelions and ragwort, securing it with the special knot and mumbled words as Abigail has shown me how to do. Abigail nods approvingly, and I experience a tiny spark of self-satisfied accomplishment.

It is short-lived.

As I place the bundle on the counter, the knot unwinds itself. The dandelions fall apart. I go to gather them up, but my touch repels them, sending them falling to the floor.

Abigail sighs.

Once I had accepted the idea I was to stay in Brell, I decided to make the best of it and learn all I could about potion-making and the healing arts. *Perhaps I could build a happy enough life here* I reasoned to myself *and find comfort and satisfaction in my work.* So I approached my apprenticeship with an enthusiasm that quickly died. For once I had found something I could not study hard enough to master.

My fumbling mind and fingers resisted teaching, while my potions boiled over, or sat murkily, refusing to heal or soothe. I mixed up the words for charms and spells, got measurements wrong, and my cauldrons burned black.

23

As for how to combine ingredients, when to harvest them, and when the right time of the moon is for picking certain flowers, I couldn't keep any of the information straight. I picked weeds instead. I lost pages of my notes.

I did manage to succeed in keeping figures accurately. Abigail had taught me to keep track of the money owed her by different families in the village, and my long lists of numbers was the only thing that made her smile with satisfaction. I told myself glumly this was only because I was good at mathematics.

Despite my obvious lack of talent, Abigail's teaching is slow and deliberate. Sometimes she loses patience, throwing her hands up in despair. She orders me to go while she cleans up whatever mess I have made of my work.

When I return she only says it is no matter. She goes into her sleeping chamber and shuts the heavy oak door with a bang, leaving me to fume.

It's been nearly two years. I should be a full healer at this point, but I am still her apprentice. Why won't she realize I am no good at this? Why is she determined to keep me here?

If I could do well at this I would, but its hopeless. Yet Abigail makes me try again and again. She stubbornly won't give up and she won't let me go.

It is late afternoon. We are standing in the kitchen of our small cottage measuring out ingredients for one of Abigail's special potions. The cauldron on the fire bubbles and glows with faint, yellow light. It lights the blackened stones set in the circular alcove of the fireplace and casts a strange glow across the hearth.

As I miserably gather up the broken dandelions Abigail shakes out a jar of chives and chops them, her knife making a familiar clicking noise on the wooden table.

The fire makes the kitchen hotter than usual. The sweat drips down my neck and forehead, and I move away from the table quickly before any drops fall.

Working with magic, one has to be cautious about any stray bead of perspiration, any floating hair, or even a particle of skin getting caught up in the charm or potion one is working.

I have learned this the hard way. A drop of my sweat landing in a mixture of coppery stuff one day and the explosion sent us running for cover. The hole it blew in the kitchen wall still hasn't been fully repaired.

The day has been unusually warm. I go to the window and open it slightly, pushing it outward with a creak. Sunshine falls on the garden and glints on the river. The sun is stretching the last of its golden rays on us as evening begins.

"It will be autumn soon," says Abigail, intent on her work, and I inhale the humid air drifting into the room, touching my face in an explorative manner.

She sighs again and I glance back over my shoulder to find her watching me, shaking her head, regretting something.

"I'll make the evening delivery for you," I offer lamely.

I have begun to find the look of speculative regret on Abigail's face more and more. Since she won't release me from my promise, I long to be away from it, out under the early evening sky.

The firelight reflects in Abigail's dark eyes, giving her the look of a small animal crouching. It vanishes as she blinks. She taps out some white powder onto the table and mixes it into a heap of wilting forget-me-not flowers. The powder turns the petals into sparkling blue glass, and she scoops this up, tossing it unceremoniously into the pot. There is a pop and the liquid turns bright blue. I watch in mild envy.

Abigail sings softly to a bit of lavender. She turns and drops the bundle of sweet-smelling herbs into the cauldron, which sparks and dissolves in a slow creep of beautiful, violet-hued liquid. Clapping the lid on the pot, she moves it slightly outward, away from the heat, where it sways gently on its iron hanger.

"Yes, I would like you to do the delivery, Thea." Abigail says, going over to an uneven wooden box and selecting three jars of raspberry colored gel glimmering with faint veins of gold.

"Only one customer tonight," she explains. "These are for the Alderberry boy. He has an unusual fever. Tell his mother to dose him three times a day with a tablespoon of this stirred into tea. Three times a day for the next fifteen days. Even when he appears to be better, she must keep up the doses, or else the fever will return."

25

I write these instructions down carefully and place the jars into my basket.

"There have more than a few strange fevers this summer," I observe, trying to sound interested.

Abigail only makes a noise with her nose. I smile wanly, and her eyes soften, the regretful expression gone as if it had never been.

"I'll be back before it is too dark," I say, suddenly irritable.

She waves to me as I go down the path to the garden gate, unlatch it, and set off down the road to the village.

By the time I have delivered the potions, given Mrs. Alderberry Abigail's careful instructions, and pocketed the precious silver coins securely in my apron, the sun has nearly set. Long shadows are thrown over the path as I hesitate, eyeing the glow of Owl's Roost.

Maggie and Thomas will be back from their honeymoon by now. They have spent it in Moor, taking in the sights and sounds of that colorful place, and I am eager to hear all they had seen and done. Torn between the growing dark and my desire to be away from Abigail and her disappointment, Owl's Roost wins.

I trot around the back of the inn and slip into the kitchen door in the old way. I run into Bol, who nearly drops the empty, dirty glasses he is carrying.

"Thea!" he exclaims. "Help me will you, there's a good girl!"

Not waiting for my response, he hands me a dishtowel and sweeps back into the noisy, crowded bar. I sigh a little but take the towel, wiping down tables and gathering up empty dishes.

I try to be as unobtrusive as possible among the groups of villagers. There is no sign of Maggie or Thomas, but near the fire sits a group of strange men and women, who eye me with interest.

"Pretty lass," says one of the older men, in a gruff tone, but by now I am artful in the way of a seasoned barmaid.

I give him a scathing look, silencing him. The other men in the group laugh, but the woman closest to me smiles at me in sympathy.

"Another round!" they call, and I hurry away from them. Behind the bar I pour the dark sweet ale.

"Maggie and Thomas aren't back yet?"

Bol comes flying back into the main room, a tray loaded with steaming cuts of meat and buttered bread balanced on his arm.

"Nay, not yet, but I'm on the watch."

He gestures at the strangers. "Didn't expect such a crowd tonight, but the weather is nice, and so it makes for good traveling."

"I can't stay long –" I begin, meaning to tell him Abigail will worry, but there is a yell from the bar, and he rushes away to fill the drained glasses.

In the corner is a shadowy figure of a man. His cloak is drawn up and his face is half hidden by his hood. It's odd because the day has been warm, and the room is warmer still.

His eyes are on me and I go over to him, scrunching my nose at the smell of him, musty and sour, like old rotting wood.

Or something dead.

I shake this thought away.

"Can I get you some more ale, sir?" I ask him, picking up his empty glass.

His fingers close on my wrist. I glance down at his hand, startled. It's beautiful.

I look into his face. He is exceptionally handsome. His features are even, his lips full and sensuous. Even the scar running lightly across his jaw only serves to make him interesting. His dark hair flops forward across his forehead, thick and full.

Good-looking or not, he is old enough to be my father and I don't like strangers touching me. I draw away indignantly.

"Wait," he says softly.

His voice makes me uncomfortable. He is staring at my chest. Not at any curves I have there, but at my Mama's necklace. I have worn it since the day she died and put it in my hand.

It's a simple necklace. A small, oval, gold pendant with a complicated lavender-colored glass 'S' set in its center. The 'S' has leaves and flowers woven around it.

As he reaches for it, it buzzes sharply against my skin and I draw back with a gasp. He drops his hand from my wrist.

"No. I suppose not."

His smile doesn't touch the rest of his face. I am apprehensive but try and hide it.

"What interesting eyes you have, child. Bol tells me you are intelligent as well?"

I am confused but assured. If this stranger knows Bol it must be all right.

"I was smart enough to clear my entrance exams for the university in Moor."

I clear away his dishes quickly, eager to move away from him. He watches me in silence.

"And when are you off to this university in Moor?"

There is something forlorn in his voice.

I hesitate. But why does it matter if I tell this stranger the truth?

"I'm not. I promised my guardian I'd stay here and be her apprentice. She makes healing potions," I finish lamely.

"It must be disappointing. A bright girl like you."

"My guardian has been kind and I promised. It's important to keep promises."

I linger reprovingly, but the man only looks at me. I walk away and when I glance over at his corner a few minutes later he is gone, only a coin or two left on the table for the ale and meal. I put him out of my head.

An hour creeps by, then a quarter of an hour. Bol sighs at last and pats my shoulder.

"Thank you, girl. I can handle it from here."

He hands me a small bag of coins as payment and I exclaim at the weight of it.

"No, no," he insists, "You've helped me out. Now be off with you before Abigail comes looking for you."

I thank him and slide out the door, intending to make my way home as quickly as possible.

As I leave the village, the road is dark. A warm mist has risen from the river until a thick coat of it lies in every direction. I go slowly, picking my way across the smooth stones of the road. Through the fog, the dark shapes of trees are standing unsteady on the riverbank.. I walk faster.

I am not afraid, but as I near Abigail's cottage a queer sort of shuddering creeps its way into my skin. The sour and musty scent weaves into my nose and freezes me where I stand.

"Good evening."

His hood is still drawn up to hide his face.

I stand still and strain to see in front of me as his tall form emerges from the mist.

"I'm leaving town," the strange man says conversationally. "Thea, is it?"

"Yes, sir."

I am uneasy, but I am steps from our cottage, and he isn't standing particularly close to me.

"Your eyes are unusual. Like mine."

I look up at him, startled. His eyes are a familiar shade of blue rimmed with gold.

"Are we related?"

But the man shakes his head. "Not at all."

Something is radiating from him. A color I had never seen. The edges of it are black smoke. The insides of it are a swirling, bright green.

Bewitched, I stare at it. I open my lips to tell him to get back, but only a faint whimper trickles out of some recess in my throat. It is enough. The color vanishes.

"Thea," says the man, as if nothing has happened. "If you want an education, you should get it."

He hands me a small sack heavy with the weight of coins.

"Oh no," I say, my shock forgotten. "I can't take this."

"Think of me as your fairy-godmother," His voice sounds as if he might laugh. "Take the path through the forest. On the other side is a main road. It will lead you to Moor. You can start your life."

"A path through the forest? But no one enters the forest."

"That's nonsense. It's perfectly safe if you stick to the path. It's just there."

He gestures with his beautiful fingers across the river beyond our cottage. There is a flash of silver in the dark trees.

I gaze at the sack full of coins. He is offering me freedom. I open my mouth to speak, to reject his offer, to give him the reasons why I can't betray Abigail. To explain I am bound by a promise. I look up into his eyes that mirror mine.

There is a burst of warm light, and my gaze is torn from the stranger to a brilliant lantern swung through misty air. Thomas's voice, rich and loud, echoes through the mist.

"Ey! Who's there?"

Some spell breaks and the frogs in the swamp below explode in a chorus.

"Thea!" Abigail is calling to me from behind Thomas.

She is standing near the gate to her cottage, swinging a small lantern back and forth, a beacon of hope and safety. Maggie stands near her, looking anxious.

"I have to go," I say, shoving the bag of coins back into the stranger's hand. "I appreciate it, but no thank you."

I dart around him. As I pass, he does not reach after me but stands perfectly still. In a moment I fling myself into Thomas's outstretched arms, clinging to his warmth and familiarity. He holds me tightly.

"Well, now!" he says happily. "Aren't you a sight!"

He raises his lantern high.

"Who goes there?"

There is no answer. Where the man has been, drifts empty darkness with only the occasional spark of tiny lights blinking here and there. There is no sign of the stranger at all.

I peer around Thomas's arm, my eyes wide, searching for him. The road is empty, as if he has never been. The frog's singing stops, like all of the creatures have leaped underwater at once.

INTO THE DARK

No one asks about the strange man I had been speaking to. Perhaps Thomas has decided he imagined it.

He and Maggie stay and visit with us. They give me some presents they have picked up in Moor. Books, sweets and fruit, a new cloak for me, fine glass vials for Abigail, and a new rug for the main room.

They talk over each other about the fine sights they have seen in the dazzling Capitol city. I am sick with envy when they talk about the crowded city streets and the enormous buildings and open markets. I ask dozens of questions and try to ignore Abigail's stiff silence.

"We saw the university when we were there," says Thomas, nudging my arm in a fond way. "It was enormous. All those students and their serious faces. I wondered how'd you'd like it –

But Maggie has kicked him sharply and he subsides, looking bewildered and embarrassed.

My ears burn and I poke the fire, unable to say anything. No one knows why I have chosen to stay in Brell and be Abigail's apprentice, but Maggie with her thoughtful intuition, senses it is a delicate subject. Abigail's brows are drawn together, and she has gotten up to get us more tea.

"No, no," Maggie puts in hastily, rising and pulling Thomas to his feet. "We must be going, Abigail."

"Must you?" Abigail is grim. "Well, be careful. There are sometimes strangers on the road."

I glance at her sharply, but her face is carefully blank.

Thomas laughs and gives me a hug, breaking a little of the

tension in the room. "No stranger on the road will bother us!"

Maggie wraps herself in her cloak and hugs me close, whispering for me to come and visit her the next day. She has a few more surprises for me.

When they have gone, the room feels empty. Abigail and I look at each other across the glow of the fire.

"You were late coming home?" she says quietly.

The question is not accusing or harsh in any way, but I have the familiar tinge of annoyance.

"I said I was helping Bol," I reply shortly.

Abigail sighs, deciding not to press it. "Tomorrow I'll need some help with inventory. Where is Ironsides?"

"In the garden perhaps."

I am surprised by her abrupt change of topic.

She rises and goes out the door, leaving it wide. I follow her and stand at the door. I look out into the empty road. Nothing there but a fog and wet. Near the gate of the cottage, Abigail leans down and pokes under the moss-covered roots of a thorny tree standing at the side of the garden path.

"Come on, Ironsides." She picks up the turtle and holds him against her.

Ironsides is staring, his eyes wide and unblinking, in the direction of the road. He appears to be smelling the air, stretching his neck long and high as turtles do.

"It's a thick mist, although you don't mind, do you?"

Abigail's voice is gentle as she carries him back toward the cottage. Ironsides is still gazing over her hand in the direction of where the stranger has been. His eyes are glinting strangely, but perhaps it is only the lantern light.

Abigail is hurrying inside and pulling me after her, shutting the door behind her, pushing the latch firm. Inside, silence envelops us again. Abigail hands Ironsides to me. I cradle him in my hands. She considers me.

"You have Cecilia's eyes."

Her tone is both hopeful and sad, and I am guilty, looking at her. Ironsides moves restlessly and I set him in my lap. Agitated, he disappears into his shell and I trace the golden lines on his back with a finger.

It must have been the talk of Moor and my obvious interest in it. She has been a mother to me, while I am ungrateful. She opens her mouth to say more, but I lean and kiss her on her weathered cheek. I don't want to apologize, but I don't want to talk about my Mama either. She is startled by my kiss. We aren't demonstrative.

"Goodnight Abigail."

I avoid her gaze and leave her standing in the middle of the main room. I climb the stairs to my small attic room and close the door behind me.

After a few minutes, there are the creak of her footsteps as she douses the fire and snuffs the lanterns. I watch the light vanishing through the cracks in my floor. Her own bedroom door closes with a soft click. Familiar nighttime silence settles on the cottage.

In my room I put Iron's headless and legless shell on my pillow and go over to a small chest. The chest had been brought with me when I had come to live with Abigail. It is worn and its straps are faded and cracking. I kneel, opening it and digging down to the side and bottom. It holds old clothes and a few old keepsakes. I find my Papa's favorite writing pen and a dried bottle of ink. A handkerchief belonging to my Mama, her initials carefully embroidered on the edge and surrounded by tiny flowers. I put these on the floor beside me. I pull out a small leather satchel and hold it carefully.

It is crumpled with age, hastily stuffed away. A faint, golden symbol is pressed into the leather. The swoop of the lines reminds me of the golden lines on Ironsides' shell.

I stretch it open and draw from it a rolled piece of parchment, tied with a bit of blue ribbon. Along with this is a carved piece of wood with three holes along the side of it and a tapered end. It is a whistle or tiny flute. As usual, I marvel at its delicate carving, bring it to my lips, and blow a soft note. The sound comes out low and echoing. It blows around the room, taps the walls, flies across the bed, and settles away into nothing. Unrolling the parchment, I examine the strange writing for the hundredth time. It is not in any language I know.

These are my Mama's things. When I was thirteen, Abigail brought them out and gave them to me.

"Perhaps they are only keepsakes," she had told me. "But they may contain some clue to your parent's past. I've never seen this kind of writing before. Perhaps it's the language of the country they came from."

I had taken the scroll to school and shown it to my teacher. Master Patterson, always encouraging, was intrigued. He gave me some books on the various languages of our country, and I searched them endlessly, but my Mama's scroll language was not among them.

Considering this, I wonder if the university in Moor has books on languages in their library. I bet they do. Hundreds.

Go and find out.

The thought comes to me as if someone else had spoken the words. I shift position and hear the clink of coins falling. I think of the stranger's sack of coins and wonder if he had managed to give them to me despite my refusal. But reaching into my skirt pocket, I realize it is the money I had earned at Owl's Roost.

Normally I would have given it to Abigail to put away for our household needs, but in the excitement of seeing Maggie and Thomas, I had forgotten.

It is my money, after all I think, trying not to feel guilty. *I earned it.* I could take the money, a little food, and go and visit the university. There is no harm in it. I wouldn't stay. I would spend a few nights in Moor and see the library and perhaps someone there could help me decipher my scroll. I could even follow the path through the forest the strange man had suggested. He had said it was quicker.

My heart is beating fast with excitement. Why have I never considered a visit before? I'm not leaving forever. For a week, perhaps.

Determined, I gather up my Papa's old inkwell and my Mama's old handkerchief and the little leather pouch. I find a small empty pack I had used in school and place these items in it. I add extra clothes and a small bottle of water. Taking out some old parchment, I hastily write a note to Abigail, explaining where I have gone and when I will return.

I can travel the night and reach the road by morning. Perhaps I could hitch a ride, or even walk. It can't be far to Moor, after all. I won't wake Abigail and tell her. She would never allow me to go by myself. Or perhaps I am worried she wouldn't allow me to go at all.

34

I am about to leave the room when there is a soft sound. Ironsides is watching me. His head has emerged from his shell and his eyes are jewel bright. I go over and pick him up and put him on my shoulder. Why not take my turtle? He would be good company for me on the road. We go to the window and gaze out across the river to the trees. The flash of the silver path is gleaming there. I wonder why I had never seen it until now.

I go out of the cottage and shut the door softly behind me. I go down the garden path. The world is wet and dripping. I turn my back on the cottage and creep down the bank to the wet length of sand, towards the step-stones laying across the shallows. I begin to slowly hop from rock to rock. I am electric with excitement. I can't believe I'm leaving.

A tiny colored light zips by my face and I am alarmed, nearly losing my balance. I regain my footing and with a swift leap, I land on the island. I pause and consider the best way of crossing the deeper water to the other side. There is no boat and the water comes up well over my head. I had learned to swim, but never liked it; the uncertainty of water and weightlessness combined with a certain blindness in one's footing. As a result, I am not a strong swimmer. I gaze out over the river. The current is moving deep and fast.

Abruptly, I am aware of a small knocking sound. It's the sound of wood bumping against wood. On the shore is a small dock and mooring post. A tiny skiff, tied up to the post, is moving with the current and bumping the wooden dock with its nose.

There doesn't appear to be anyone about, but this little boat must belong to someone. Puzzled, I hurry down to it and examine it carefully. It is empty except for two small oars. It appears to be an ordinary skiff, flat-bottomed with a square stern and a pointed bow.

I borrow it. I climb inside it and unstrap the oars, fitting them in the rowlocks. It is easy for me to dip the blades into the water and pull back. The boat shoots off from the bank and I am in the current. The strength of the river tugs at the wood under my feet.

The mist on the river is dense and as I pull into mid-stream, the shores on both sides disappear. For a moment I am lost in a strange white world. Determined, I keep rowing.

The stern grinds against the pebbled bank, and I leap out of the skiff awkwardly, wetting my boots and the hem of my dress. Leaving the little craft on the sand, I hope that whoever its owner is, they are not put out by my use of it.

I don't glance back. If I had I might have seen the boat fade into the darkness as if it had never been. Instead I scramble up the bank and find myself a step or two away from the thick trees. The flow of water behind me is the only sound.

Stepping into the trees, I stand carefully for some minutes, keeping my breath even, listening for any sound. The trees smell strange, like ice or cool water in a cave and in a flash I remember being here before when I was much younger. It is darker than I have ever known it to be. My eyes have not adjusted. I can only see the forest floor and the shadow of tangled undergrowth.

There it is as the man said, a smooth path of silver dust, laying between the trees. More of the funny colored lights zip along it, leading me forward.

I leave the river and the edge of the forest behind, and I am relaxed. The trees are protective, not menacing. There are small rustling night sounds of tiny forest creatures. Nothing alarms me until a rabbit dodges across my path, and I jump and nearly fall. Before I can recover a shrill whistle pierces the air.

I freeze and stare around wildly but see no one. Around my neck the 'S' in my Mama's golden necklace glows, but I don't perceive it.

All is silent.

A bird's whistle I think, calming slightly, but the whistle comes again, this time long and low and teasing in my ear. There is a silence as it fades away. Nothing moves in the undergrowth. No wind stirs the leaves above me.

But the insistent sound comes a third time, dying faintly on the air, moving away. Is it only a bird? It sounds strangely like speech. If I listen carefully I might be able to distinguish words in it.

A noise rustles the dim greenery, and turning my head to follow it, I go hot and cold. There is someone there among the trees, whistling to me. Shaking, I take a step toward the shadow off the silvery path.

I am thinking of my Papa, the weight of his gentle hand on my hair for the last time. I whisper his name, not hearing my own voice, nor the childish whimper following it.

Behind me something moves silently against the depth of trees. It rises and turns into the tall figure of a man in a dark cloak. But I see nothing, staring into the dark, looking for – what?

There is a flash of light as bright as the sun. It lights up the trees on all sides of me. I shield my eyes and cower where I am unable to move. A scream rips through the air. Dark shadows, leaving trails of whirling leaves, come from nowhere and rush past me disappearing into the underbrush.

Bewildered and terrified I turn to run, but the ground beneath my feet rocks and sways. I cannot keep my balance. There is a deafening crack and I gaze, open-mouthed at a great tree rushing towards me as if it has grown legs.

Impossible. The tree reaches out a heavy branch and strikes me from my feet. I am falling into searing fire, and thick earth, and I remember nothing more.

IRONSIDES

When I open my eyes, I find myself alone, lying on the roots of a great oak tree. I sit up, my head spinning, and I try to sort out what has happened. For a few minutes, I can't remember anything except vague flashes. Trees, shadows, mist and – hissing?

I rub my head where it aches. The silver path is gone, even though I was only steps from it. There is nothing but trees and hanging moss in all directions. Faint morning sunlight slants through branches. I am all alone inside a strange, wooded world.

"Where am I?" I whisper into the silence.

I do not cry but am dizzy and sick. Rubbing my head again, I try to piece together what happened. I remember the little boat, walking the silver path, the strange whistling and the tree that had grown legs.

It all is so much like a dream I want to laugh, but I am wide-awake. I shake my head, glancing at the trees around me. They are ordinary trees, although unusually large.

It's absurd. But if so, how was I knocked out? I touch my head gingerly and discover a small bump, as well as a shallow cut. I lick my fingers and rub it again. A faint pink stain comes off on my hand. Blood.

I search for my pack and find it near me. Everything is still there, the food, my Mama's mysterious scroll and flute, and the extra clothing. Ironsides is a sleeping shell with no head or legs. He is laying near where my head lay, determined to guard me. I pick him up and put him in my pocket. I take out a piece of bread and a small bottle of water. These make me feel better, though my head still aches.

Putting the pack on my shoulder I stand up, looking around. There is nothing to indicate which direction I should go. I decide to follow a way that is less crowded with trees and underbrush than the other. As I walk I take everything in. I didn't know the forest looked like this.

Most of the trees are at least twenty feet wide. Passing one is like walking around a small house. Their branches hang low, covered in white lichen and wisps of Spanish moss. The ground beneath my feet is a soft carpet of dead undergrowth. Sometimes bushes and brambles block the way and I go around these, taking care not to touch them. When I pass they shift slightly in invisible winds. The tree branches above my head creak eerily, but down on the ground the air is still. There are no sounds of birds or small animals. There is perfect silence except for the faintest stir in the air or the motion of a plant as I pass.

"As if they were alive," I say aloud. "As if they could hear, think, speak, and feel."

I hurry, glancing behind me from time to time. There is nothing there, but there is a prickly sensation on the back of my neck I can't ignore. Reaching up, I touch my oval-shaped necklace, warm around my neck.

Slanting through the towering trees, the light is soft green in color. It turns the edges of the green leaves golden. There are other lights hovering around the branches above my head. These are the strange colored lights of last night, and they swoop in front of me and weave glimmering patterns in the air. I unconsciously follow them. They zip away into the trees, zoom back and circle around me, only to fly away again after a moment.

Hours later, the sun slants through the trees and fades to a dim gold. I pause to untangle a strand of my hair from an aggressive thorn bush. The branch had reached out and grasped my hair with a determined tug. By this time I am accustomed to the strange movement of the trees and brambles and am more annoyed than frightened. Hot and tired, I fight with the persistent thorny branch. As I do, a new sound begins to trickle into my ears.

Giving my hair a final yank, the branch snaps back unexpectedly, setting me free. I have drunk the last of my water hours ago and follow the noise eagerly. I break through the thicket to find myself in a glade with slender birch trees. A clear spring winds through them, bubbling over mossy stones.

With a groan of relief I kneel down on the grassy bank and scoop water up with my hands. It is cold and sweet. I bath my face and my arms in it.

There is a small movement in my pocket, and I pull Ironsides out. His face is sleepy, and he blinks at me. I set him down in the soft moss near the edge of the stream and scoop up some water in my palm.

"There you are," I say, pouring it over his shell.

The turtle stretches out his neck. In the sunshine slanting through the trees, the golden marks on his shell glow.

I stare at him, "You look bigger."

"I expect I am bigger," he says.

I give a shriek and sit back on my heels.

"What?" I gasp, trying to catch my breath, "What did you *say*?"

"Sorry. I could not speak to you before, not in that horrid place. The air around Brell took my voice away. I have been nearly an ordinary turtle for fifteen years." He gives a snort of disgust and claws the ground. "I was afraid sometimes it was starting to affect my mind."

My own mind is whirling, "Am I dreaming?"

Ironsides gives me a serious look. "You are not. You have come home is all."

He stretches his head again and slaps his tail on the ground. "We both have."

"Home? This is home?"

"It is," says the turtle, gazing around curiously, "and the forest has woken up. It is a particularly good sign."

He turns around to face me.

"Welcome home, Princess Althea Luna Elizabeth Celia Morgan."

There is the hint of a grin about his dour mouth.

His words don't register, then I find my voice.

"Princess? What?"

The turtle lifts a clawed foot at me.

"Be quiet for a moment, will you? *Waters!*" he calls the last word loudly and I blink.

I look around at the stream. "Do you want more –?" I begin, but Ironsides shushes me and there is a brief silence.

"WATERS!" yells the turtle again, much louder, and again I am about to scoop another handful of water for him when there is a small popping sound, like a plug being pulled from a drain.

I look around me again. The endless maze of trees sits waiting. There is nothing but a green and gold shadowy silence. The tiny lights are skimming over the water in graceful arches. I glance down at the spring.

There in the mud is one of the strangest creatures I have ever seen. It appears to be nothing but eyes the color of the shifting stream bed. I wouldn't have noticed them if they hadn't blinked up at me, disappearing and reappearing in a slow motion. The rest of the creature is made of mud. Its form moves with the flow of water, at first perfectly round and then resembling a spatter of ink on a page.

I am leaning over to get a better look when all at once the creature rises up from the muddy bank and regards me curiously. This is unexpected and I let out a startled scream.

The creature immediately makes a muddy opening near its eyes and says, "Hush!"

I am so shocked to hear it speak I sit back on my heels and am silent.

The creature's mouth widens in what appears to be a friendly way.

"That's right. That's the way. Keep quiet and he won't know you're here."

I look from the thing to my turtle, my head spinning, and decide I'm having a hallucination. The creature bobs up and down, growing wider and shorter in the shallow water. It turns to Ironsides.

"Hullo Iron!" it says cheerfully, "Nice to have you back!"

"Hullo Waters."

The turtle is calm, as if sand with eyes is a natural thing.

"Where have you been?"

"Busy, but I got here as fast as I could." He jerks his sandy form up and down in the shallow water. "I might have been here earlier, but I was sidetracked by Broon."

"Where is he? I would have thought he'd be here to meet us."

"No, no. He's busy now, but he sends his best and says to expect him tonight."

The creature turns to me politely.

"Are you all right your Highness?"

I don't answer, staring at the creature in bewilderment.

"She doesn't know," says the turtle, chewing on some leaves. "No one told her."

"She doesn't know?"

"No, but it's too long to explain now. Let's be off, shall we?" The turtle looks around the small glade. "I don't want to stay in one place too long."

I find my voice and it comes out loud and high-pitched.

"Where am I? And what it is it I don't know?"

The turtle and the strange sand creature stare at me. Finally the sand creature chuckles, sending a spatter of mud across the water.

"This is Thornwold. This is the Forest of Thornwold, often called the Thorn. After this, there's the chasm and beyond that Castle Stoneham, and further still there are the Light and Dark Mountains covered in snow and ice. These stretch down to the Glasshedge Moors and away to the Glass Sea, but I've not been so far. I prefer to stick to the Thorn and to the caverns."

My head whirls with this information and I sink back, sitting on the cold grassy bank. The thing bends forward and makes ripples in the water. It examines its own reflection and my pale face.

"What - who are you?" I falter.

The turtle gives a snort. "He's a nuisance, most of the time."

The creature shakes his muddy body, giving the turtle a narrow look. He draws himself up proudly.

"I'm William Waters. But you can call me Will. Or Waters. I'm a Mudgluck. There are many of us, though not so many in your world." He twists sharply, spattering more of his muddied self around and I dodge a spray of mud.

"How did I get here?" I demand, looking from Ironsides to the Mudgluck, "I heard whistling –"

"Hush!" Will turns serious. "Don't speak about it now! Ember will explain. Come now, we mustn't stay here. It isn't safe. You've been stumbling around here attracting the attention of who knows what. I guess it's a good thing they've been leading you."

He motions with his eyes rather scornfully towards the flickering lights, now dancing in wide circles around us in the gathering gloom.

I am momentarily distracted and delighted to find the lights so close to me at last. I put out my hand. One of the lights lands on my wrist, and I can make out the silvery form of a tiny figure. It is shaped something like a human with over-sized dark eyes, butterfly wings, and slender feelers protruding from its tiny head. I take all this in before the other lights surround me in a cloud of colors. The softest sensation is running through me, making my lips and cheeks burn.

"Now – now," sputters Will, "Enough!"

He flings a bit of water through the lights and they scatter back into their circles. A sound comes from them: the faintest ringing of bells. One of them swoops down and perches itself on Ironsides shell. He gives a jump of annoyance and it rolls off into a patch of moss.

"What are they?" I ask dazedly. "Are they fairies?"

"Fairies?" Ironsides scoffs, "Everyone knows there's no such thing."

I blink at this, but Will explains, "They are the Quickwillow. When they get close to you, they do make one a bit dizzy-like." He peers around us with his sandy eyes, "We should be off. It isn't a bit safe here, your Highness."

"That's another thing. Why do you keep calling me Highness? My name is Thea. I'm not a Highness."

The little mud man looks at Ironsides helplessly, but the turtle clears his throat. "Thea, your parents were King and Queen of Thornwold. You are their daughter. You are the Princess."

"No. No. It can't be. We've always lived in Brell."

"Your parents haven't."

I put my head in my hands and shut my eyes tight. This is a dream. It must be a dream. But when I lift my head, Ironsides is still standing there and so is Will Waters the Mudgluck. The Quickwillow dart about me anxiously.

The turtle eyes me. "Thea, I would never lead you to danger. I have been protecting you since you were born. We have to go see Ember. She will help us and explain everything. It's an exceedingly long story."

I don't move.

The Mudgluck makes a noise like water gurgling down the

drain. "I forgot."

His eyes disappear into the muddy bank. In a moment, he reappears and spits an object out onto the grass. "My token."

I pick up the object, scrape it off, and give a cry. A silver-framed miniature portrait of a much younger Cecilia Morgan smiles up at me.

"Where did you get this? This is my Mama. How did you get this?"

The creature has straightened itself out of the mud until it is over a foot tall. "Ember gave it to me for you." He is sure this explains everything.

"Who is Ember?"

But Iron has crept up onto my lap and nudges my hand, "Come on, my darling. We can't stay here."

His voice is patient, like someone speaking to a person who is ill or unreasonable. I stare down at the age-worn portrait. I stare back at the little mud-man and down at my turtle.

"Fine. We'll go see this Ember. But I want answers."

"And you will get them," assures Ironsides.

I pick him up and he waves his feet a bit indignantly.

Will Waters laughs. "That's new, Iron. You never let anyone pick you up. You must be getting soft."

The turtle gives a snort but says nothing.

"Do you mind it?" I ask him. "You never said."

"I couldn't say," he reminds me. "But no, not when it's you. You or your parents. You three are different."

I set him on my shoulder and slip the portrait into my pocket, I rise to my feet. I smile at the mud-creature.

"I'm Thea."

The Mudgluck widens his mouth in a smile.

"I know." He bends his body over towards the water until his eyes are level with the surface. I realize he is bowing.

"Come on," says Ironsides, a bit irritably. "This isn't a social tea. You've already met. Let's get going."

Will straightens up and shrinks back until he is a few inches tall. He looks me over doubtfully. "You can't travel as I do. I go underground. You'll have to follow the stream and the Quickwillow. I'll be nearby if you need help. Are you afraid?"

"No." I'm not, but I am tired. My legs ache.

"She has *me*," emphasizes the turtle, sounding put out.

"How long until we get there?" I ask, but the Mudgluck is gone.

"Not long," Ironsides nudges my cheek with his head. "This way."

He motions to the Quickwillow, who are winding around me and pushing me forward with tiny hands.

The glade is sinking into deep green shadows now as the sun fades. I follow the spring down a slope. It vanishes into a thick layer of undergrowth.

"Here I go," I say to no one in particular, and reaching a hand into my pocket, I clutch my mother's portrait as a talisman. I plunge into the thicket, and a moment or two later nothing can be heard in the glade except the sound of flowing water.

After a little, the moon comes out and lingers on the shining spring and the muddy bank. It casts forest shadows on the green turf. A sound detaches itself from the noise of water. A sharp whistle, eerie and ominous, shrills a warning through the soft air.

The hooded figure makes no noise as he moves into the glade. A strange smell, musty and ancient, surrounds him. He flings a silver and pink arc from his fingers. The arc swirls around the place where Thea had been sitting and comes back to him. He catches it deftly. He raises his fingers and touches them to his mouth, breathing in something only he can sense. He smiles.

UNDERGROUND

I push my way through bracken and thicket for hours. Sometimes I am forced to wade deep into the middle of the spring where the rushing water tears at my legs, pushing me off balance. The cloud of butterfly winged Quickwillow fly around me, leaving interesting trails of light on the air.

Ironsides, perches on my shoulder, digging his claws slightly into my skin, but not so hard it hurts. He says nothing. Every so often, he nips my ear gently in encouragement.

I walk on, stumbling with weariness. I want to drop from exhaustion, and the many colors of the Quickwillow are swimming before my eyes when I come to a small clearing.

Here, the forest widens into a circle of great trees. The spring turns into a leaping tumble of water. It pours over a ravine and down into a deep pool. The Quickwillow rapidly drop from the air and dive as one, a blur of color, into the pool.

Blinking in the darkness, I make my way carefully down the ravine, slipping once or twice on wet rocks, and stand still at the edge of the water. The darkness is heavy and the mist from the waterfall is curiously warm.

From out of the roar of water, a clear, beautiful, voice says, "Open the door!"

The waterfall becomes a trickle as the rock behind it swings soundlessly open on invisible hinges. A dim golden light spills from the opening, and Ironsides gives me a nudge.

"Go on," he says in my ear.

"How?"

The pool is deep. Hesitantly, I put out one foot.

To my surprise, the water turns solid when I touch it. It is as hard as stone and smooth as glass. I step out onto it. I shuffle across and climb the steps to the doorway on the other side. Peering inside, my eyesight gradually adjusts to the dim light.

A tall woman with long, dark hair is standing inside the door. Her face and bare arms are faintly tinged with red and gold, as if a million pieces of colored glass have been crushed into a fine dust and sprinkled onto her skin. Her face is unlined and smooth, but streaks of silver fly up from her temples.

"Come in," she says in a slightly accented voice, "Please come in."

I step inside and the door swings shut behind me. The color that hovers around her is faint, a mix of orange and gold. Sparks flitter from her as she moves. She smiles at me warmly.

"You must be Ember," I say awkwardly. I wasn't sure what I had been expecting, but it wasn't this beautiful woman. I am conscious of how small I am in comparison, of my dirt stained clothes and tangled hair, but Ember doesn't appear to notice.

"This is such an honor. I have waited many years to meet you." She offers me her hand.

I take the offered hand and there is a slight jolt of heat, as our fingers touch. I jump.

She reaches out and presses the tip of her fingers to Ironsides' shell. "Ironsides."

"Hullo Ember. It's been a long time."

"So it has. Too long."

The woman smiles at the turtle and to my surprise, she has tears in her eyes. Turning, she claps her hands. Sconces spring to life, the bright fire licking up the stone walls.

As she moves to stand next to me, I breathe in her scent. She smells like fire and smoke, but not unpleasantly. Something about it reminds me of Abigail's cottage or Owl's Roost, and I swallow a pang of homesickness.

Emerging from the shadows in the passageway are a group of tiny people, eyeing me carefully. They are all dressed in the same muddy colors, with low, round caps covering their heads. Their faces are the same color as the stone walls around them. The color emerging from them is the color of red earth touched with water. A taller one stands in the front. He winks at me slowly with eyes the color of sand and rock.

I grin in recognition.

"These are the –" says the woman, turning and motioning to the little people, but I interrupt.

"The Mudgluck."

Ember's dark eyes smile into mine. "They are among the oldest people of the caverns."

She is still holding my hand, the tiny jolts of electricity a pleasant buzz on my skin. She turns to the group of little people.

"May I present Her Royal Highness, Princess Althea Luna Elizabeth Cecilia Morgan."

The people bow gracefully to me as one, except Will, who bobs up and down excitedly. He is a bit younger than the others. His face is less the color of stone and more the color of sand.

At the introduction, questions are boiling in me again. This time I am determined to get answers. I step back from the woman, forcing her to drop my hand.

"I don't understand," I say, my voice coming out sharper than I mean it to. "Who am I? What am I doing here? Who were my parents?"

The woman's eyebrows raise but before she can speak, Iron clears his throat.

"She doesn't know the story, Ember. You'll have to tell her."

"You did not? They never?"

She sounds incredulous, as Will did.

"I could not," says the turtle waspishly. "And Cecilia and Douglas were protecting her."

There is an awkward pause. Ember turns to me, searching for the right words.

"Your mother and father were Queen Cecilia and King Douglas of Thornwold, and when the crown was stolen from their family by – by an interloper, they fled to my caverns. From here they went to Brell and were hidden away for many years."

My voice is angry and near tears. "But why? Why did they never tell me? Why did Abigail not know? None of this makes any sense!"

Ember is taken aback, at a loss for what to say. I hear myself being horrible and rude, but my head is spinning. The idea I've been lied to all of my life is making me furious. The Mudgluck people are watching me curiously. Only Will Waters has a look of sympathy.

The anger is hot and intense, and it takes over. In front of my eyes rises the image of myself, shunned at school and laughed at by the villagers in Brell. I see Abigail's disappointed face and my father walking away from me under the stars.

"I have been stuck in Brell my whole life. Always the outsider and always alone! And now you are telling me my parents were some kind of royalty? I'm some kind of princess? This is ridiculous! What is this about? I have lost everything! And everyone!"

A sob rips at me. Even as I say it I know the last part isn't strictly true. I still have people who love me. Maggie. Bol. Abigail. Ironsides has always been there. Proving it, Iron's voice is loud and reproving.

"Thea!"

But Ember shakes her head at him, her face is pained. "No. Thea has a right to be angry. She deserves to know it all."

She turns to me anxiously. "I don't know why they never told you, Thea. Perhaps there wasn't time. Perhaps your parent's thought you were too young. When they elected never to come back here –"

Ember stops, swallowing something.

"I'm sorry. It was a shock. When they decided not to return." Her voice is trembling. "I was close with your mother. We were girls together and you – you look so like her."

A tear glitters on Ember's cheek. I am ashamed, my outburst over. I reach up and wipe the tear away. It burns on my skin like fire, and I look down at my finger in surprise.

"I am the Lady of Fire," Ember pushes my hand away and makes a sound resembling a laugh. "My tears burn - not too badly I hope."

I'm sorry," I say awkwardly, wiping my own tears away. "But I don't understand. I need to know the whole story."

"And you will! I promise. But may we eat and rest first? I am sure you must be tired."

She's right. I am exhausted.

Ember motions at the Mudglucks, who are holding small torches and moving off down the passageway in a group. We follow them.

Ironsides sits still on my shoulder, his head half withdrawn into his shell, but his eyes stare out in front of us. He appears to be lost in thought. I pat him hesitantly, and he nudges my fingers. I am forgiven.

We walk along the passageway and I study the sparkle of gemstones buried in the rock wall. They give off a faint glimmer as the glow of torches passes over them. Ember's dark head bobs in front of me. She moves along the passage silently. Her red gown sliding along the floor reminds me of the way flame licks wood.

We haven't gone very far along the dark tunnel when we turn a corner and the passage ends abruptly. A brilliant white light is shining on us as we step out of the doorway, and I gasp.

The place we step into is an enormous cavern. The path beneath us has become a bridge made entirely of solid crystal. Around us, walls shine with precious stones. Beneath our feet, a glowing river of lava flows, bubbling hot. I have never imagined anything like it. Everywhere is glowing with incandescence, sparkle, and rich color.

I blink my eyes as golden dust floats through the air. It lands on my face and hair, but to my surprise it doesn't bother me. I put out my hand experimentally and shake it. The dust flakes off my skin and floats away, only to be replaced by more.

"What is it?" I ask, brushing at my arm before giving up.

Ironsides sneezes loudly and a puff of dust explodes near my ear.

Ember smiles. "Fallout magic dust."

"Fallout?"

"I am a bit allergic," sniffs Ironsides. "The dust has never agreed with me."

'The Thorn is full of magic," explains Ember. "It leaves a trace."

The road turns and slopes into a wide, shallow stair. Ember and I walk down it, the little band of Mudglucks leading the way. As they go along, the river of lava comes thundering past us in a golden waterfall of flame. To my surprise it is not hot, only pleasantly warm.

When I exclaim over this, Ember motions with her arm as we

go by, explaining the lava is ⬛
keep the heat at bay.

"But it does not do to tamper ⬛
only did this bit since it is so close t⬛

Below us lies a wide, white valley f⬛
trees have golden and silver wrought lea⬛
they have been carved out of ice and diam⬛
a story I had once read, about twelve princess⬛
a witch's secret cavern and wear their shoes out⬛
night.

When I say this, Ember smiles.

"This is a secret cavern. But as for the witch, well, t⬛
a few parts wrong I believe."

"Surely it was only a story? A child's tale?" I gape at her⬛

"All stories come from someplace."

The long, slow-moving lava river quiets, running through the
center of the valley and tumbling down a steep hillside into a vast,
deep lake. The lava in the lake melts into watery gold so clear, I
can see where crystal coral lays on the bottom growing in bright
colors. Shadows swim through it in quick, nimble motions.

"Fish!" I exclaim, but Ember shakes her head.

"No, Mer-people. The lake is something like water. They can
live in it."

The Mer-people swim and play about in the bright shallows of
the lava-lake. They are small and green-skinned, with tangled hair
and magnificent silver tails. The color emerging from them is
white and shot with bubbles. In the light, it turns rainbow.

Cottages made of colored stone sit on the opposite bank. In
front of these are crowds of people hurrying about, talking to one
another, and calling out greetings. They are ordinary looking, like
Brell people. Beyond the cottages is a large, marble house with a
wide veranda. Past the house are tall, sapphire hills. Streaks of
gold, like frozen shooting stars, lay on their smooth surfaces.

There is a faint ringing noise from overhead. High above our
heads, the rocky ceiling is hung with massive stalactites, each of
them crusted with glowing jewels and veins of silver and gold. The
roots of the great trees of the forest of Thornwold tangle around
them.

Among these rocks and roots are thousands of oddly shaped

own. When a
realize they

wers and

:e their
·ther, but

t."

Ve will
› my
waiting

ss, but

en you

protected by a barrier spell, helping to

with it too much," she says. "I

o where we often walk."

led with crystal trees. The

es. They look as though

nds. It reminds me of

es forced to travel to

by dancing all

he story got

_ ...on t like people staring
·, ...ut I'm not sure I want to be introduced
_. strangers as the Princess. What does it mean exactly? I
thought we were going to have something to eat and sit down in a
small room somewhere and talk. Ember and Iron and me. I
didn't think I was going to be paraded before a crowd.

"Ember?" I begin, trying to sound calm, but we are
approaching the wide, glowing river and she is a few strides ahead
of me.

"You must meet Lucius," the Lady of Fire is saying. "He is my
prized possession and loyal friend."

I am distracted from the worry of being introduced as I puzzle
how someone named Lucius can be both a possession and a
friend. The turtle on my shoulder groans loudly, making me jump.
He withdraws his head into his shell.

"Now Iron," scolds Ember, trying to hide the laughter in her
voice, "Lucius has been especially important to our cause."

"He knows it, too," grumbles the turtle from inside his shell.
"If he asks, I'm asleep."

He makes a noise like a snort, and mutters something sounding
like 'the pompous ass' but I'm not sure if I heard it right.

Straddling the river is a bridge, carved with great care to resemble a large dragon. Its back is the bridge while its great claws grip the banks and its head twists around, hanging over the flowing lava.

As we step onto it, the bridge gives a great heave. I am nearly thrown from my feet, but Ember holds my hand tightly. Several of the Mudglucks are thrown to the ground. With a great deal of swearing and shouting, they tumble about the 'bridge' knocking each other down and helping each other up in a storm of confusion.

Ember and I manage to skip quickly to the other side. We leap to the bank as the bridge-dragon stands up and stretches its enormous wings.

"Lucius!" says Ember a bit ruefully, as I rub my knee where a Mudgluck had rolled into me with a rocky thud. "We were going to cross first."

The bridge-dragon turns its great head to look at us, folding its wings back towards its body with a crash.

"I am sorry, my Lady, but I did want to pay my respects to her Royal Highness."

He turns his gaze on me, and I can't help staring open-mouthed. The dragon is made of silver and he has rubies for eyes.

"Impressive, am I not?" The dragon ruffles his silver scales, so they clink together. "None like me anywhere!"

I reach out to stroke the ridge of one of the creature's scales.

"I have always imagined dragons to be green and breathing fire. I have never seen a metal dragon."

The dragon ruffles up its scales and says haughtily, "Metal! I should think not! Child, I am made from the finest living silver, which is different from regular silver. Regular silver does not breathe or speak. Living silver is pure silver. Deep in mines near the heart of the world, silversmiths gather living silver and care for it by keeping it in bottles and jars. They grow it and feed it, and when the living silver is old enough, they carve beautiful objects from it. These objects breathe from the moment they are finished and are given great purpose and destiny."

There is a soft snort from my shoulder.

"I was made hundreds of years ago and given the task of serving the Lady of Fire. I am Lucius, the only one of my kind ever made."

The dragon bows his immense head, and I hasten to apologize.

"Of course I should have known it was living silver. How silly of me. You have such a lovely shine and beautiful rubies for eyes. I have never seen any dragon so beautiful."

I think it best not to add I had never seen a dragon at all and had never considered the possibility of their real existence.

At my praise, Lucius puffs up a bit, his scales standing out from his body and his ruby eyes glow.

"I thank you, your Highness."

When we are out of earshot, Ember says, "Lucius takes great pride in his position and appearance, but he is loyalty itself. You mustn't mind his self-important way."

"I don't. He's wonderful!" I mean this sincerely. The dragon is extraordinary.

"Destiny!" snorts the turtle from inside his shell, "Important tasks! He was your birthday gift!"

Ember and I laugh.

"He is interesting though, Iron," I tease him.

There is another derisive noise. "Be careful you don't tell him that. We'll never hear the end of it."

Ember takes my hand and leads me up the crystal path to the beautiful white house. As we near the wide staircase, crowds of people line up on either side. Men, women, and children are dressed simply in tunics or plain dresses. Many of them bow low as we approach, and Ember smiles at them as she and I go past.

Everyone is looking at me, but I forget to be nervous as the color comes swirling from them in waves. Most of it is soft yellow with traces of gold. Purple floats through some of it. Happy. Love. Pride. I smile at them shyly.

Some of the men are dressed as soldiers, in thick woolen tunics and boots. They wear sheathed swords at their waists and have stern faces. A group of these men stand near the top of the staircase. As Ember and I mount the steps, one of them steps forward.

To my surprise, he is a young man a little older than I am. He wears a dark jacket and darker tunic. His black hair falls over his forehead. His eyes go over me. Something quick and bright I can't read gleams in their depths.

The color coming from him startles me. It is no color I have ever seen. A curious mix dark gray and green with touches of silver. Not veins of silver like the sickly color of fear I remember from the long-ago day in the schoolyard, but a brighter silver. Instead it's pure, like Lucius's silver scales. I don't know what it means: the rich gray green the hue of the depths of the river in sunshine. Sorrow. Pain. I am puzzled.

He speaks to Ember, bowing low.

"There is news from above. She was followed. It is possible he is aware of her Highness's presence here."

He glances at me again and I look away in unexpected irritation. He talks about me as if I'm not there, and while he doesn't exactly glare at me, he doesn't smile either. He is looking at me the way Ironsides looks at Will, necessary, but not particularly important and rather a nuisance.

Ember is troubled. "It is to be expected. But there's little we can do about it. Don't worry, Jack, we are safe enough for the moment."

"Who's aware I'm here?" I ask, but the turtle has stretched his head out from his shell.

"Can it be Jack? Jack whom was only a baby when I left?"

Jack looks at the turtle, his face serious. "Hello Ironsides – sir," he says, adding the 'sir' jumpily, as if the turtle might reprimand him.

Ironsides looks him over, his face curious. "Well, Jack. You have grown."

The turtle's tone is odd. He sounds surprised and not best pleased at finding Jack not a baby anymore.

Jack's face flushes and I have a vision of a schoolboy in front of an old, stern schoolmaster.

"I have, sir."

"Well, it's good to see you – *here*," says the turtle in a doubtful way, putting special emphasis on the last word.

"I have been *here* for two years now," Jack answers, still more quietly, returning the emphasis. There is an edge to his voice, daring the turtle to say more.

"Jack was wounded, Ironsides," Ember puts in. "He and our other soldiers were attacked, and Jack barely survived."

She eyes the turtle severely. "Many others did not survive. I myself brought Jack here. He is welcome here as long as he wishes."

"I was only saying it was nice to see the boy," the turtle says grumpily. "No offense, lad."

Jack's voice is amused. "None taken, sir."

"By the way, where is Broon?" asks Ironsides lazily, turning away from Jack to Ember.

"He was called away," says Jack shortly, before Ember can speak. "On business of his own," he finishes pointedly, looking at Ironsides.

The turtle gives Jack a haughty look. "I was speaking to Ember. And I think I know more of these matters than you, Jack."

Jack is about to retort, but Ember interrupts. "Come now, boys! Enough of this! If we don't trust one another, where will we be?"

She takes my hand. "Come on, Thea. You must be tired and hungry."

She looks at the turtle, perched on my shoulder and still glowering at Jack, who has turned his back and is saying something to a stern-looking gray-haired man on his left.

"Coming Iron?" Her tone is a bit mocking.

Iron is furious as he glares at Ember. "Of course I'm coming! Where else would I be going?" He withdraws huffily into his shell.

Ember moves to my other side, away from the turtle, and whispers in my ear. "Iron has always been protective of the royal family. He is like a loyal watchdog. You've seen the gold painted on his shell? It is what remains of the royal crest of Stoneham. He has been in your family a long, long time."

"It's what Mama said. So Iron is a sort of royal mascot?"

"At this point, yes. But perhaps it is best not to suggest it to him. Turtles live to be incredibly old and wise. He is suspicious of anyone he considers a threat to the royal family."

"But why should he be suspicious of Jack? He is your friend, isn't he?"

"I trust Jack. But remember, Iron has been away many years and – " She pauses and goes on carefully. "Jack has an unfortunate family history. I am not sure it's my place to share it with you. I hope he will tell you himself someday."

She smiles at me, as I frown over my shoulder at the young

man. "He doesn't look much older than me."

"No," says Ember. "He isn't."

She turns into a doorway and I follow. We enter a long, beautiful room. Huge pillars run the length of it. Jeweled torches light the interior with a dazzling light. Open French doors lead to a balcony overlooking the strange lava lake. In the middle of the hall is an enormous table set with more food than I have ever imagined.

On it are steaming dishes of roasted meat. Fresh-baked bread drips with butter. Wedges of soft cheese lay next to fresh cut melon. Lemon slices float in pitchers of ice-cold water.

A small tree growing through a hole in the center of the table is laden with fruit of every kind. One side grows apples, the other pears, and another side is dropping dusty plums. There are desserts of every kind. Chocolate cake, fruit pies with cream, and tarts laden with strawberries. There are baked apples, honey-ham, biscuits with honey, and pots of tea.

Ember sits down at the head of the table. She motions me to sit at her right. A footman, splendidly dressed, steps forward bringing me hot towels and scented water. I hesitantly use them to wash my hands. When I have finished, I find the room filled with people, the same simply dressed people I had seen outside. I am not sure how the table is able to accommodate all of them, but it does.

The turtle is still perched on my shoulder, his head withdrawn.

"Do you want to eat?" I take him up and set him on the white tablecloth.

Iron puts his head and feet out and gazes around. "I'll take some of the lettuce," He indicates a large bowl.

I scoop up a few leaves of lettuce and some cut vegetables and place these in front of him. He nibbles gently, looking carefully around him between bites. I find a small figure on my right. The figure gives me a wink.

"Will!"

But the Mudgluck hushes me, signaling me to be silent, for Ember has risen gracefully to her feet. My apprehension returns. She's going to introduce me and what on earth am I supposed to say? My face turns red.

She speaks slowly and her words don't register with me at first.

57

"Friends, today is the day that turns the tide. We welcome the rightful ruler of Thornwold, the Princess Althea Luna Elizabeth Cecilia Morgan!" She pauses. "She has come back to us after twenty years to reclaim the throne that was stolen from her! We will have victory at last!"

The world has muffled to a slow roar. I am staring at Ember, open-mouthed. What has she said? I try to speak, but the room erupts in cheers and shouts. I can barely hear anything over the pounding of my heart and the rush of blood in my veins. But Will is nudging me and I clamber to my feet.

All around me are faces shining toward me with affection. As the applause grows, I see Jack across from me, half risen from his seat, as if to come to my aid if I fall. I grit my teeth and turn toward the rest of the people. Used to being glared at with suspicion, the amount of smiling faces now turned in my direction is overwhelming.

Will is nudging me again. "Bow," he hisses.

I manage a bow, but my head is pounding. Ember smiles at the crowd. "Now. Everyone feast and celebrate. Tomorrow there will be great preparations."

Everyone cheers again and falls on the food with enthusiasm.

I sit down with a thump, appetite gone, and look at Iron, who is furious. Will is anxious and strained. Jack is striding toward Ember.

Ember isn't looking at me. Her lovely face is turned resolutely away.

MALIUS

When I wake, I am still exhausted.

I am lying on a soft bed staring at a fire burning low in a grate. This is the only light in a shadowy room. Next to me, nestled in a velvety pillow, Iron's shell bumps gently against my head. A faint snore rises from it. I nudge him aside and sit up.

An ornately decorated door leading out onto a small balcony stands open. A gentle wind comes through it and brings the faint sounds of laughter and piping music. Getting up, I go to the door and step out onto the white crystal terrace.

It is nearing dawn, though how I know this I can't say since all I have to measure it by is the faint glow of the Quickwillow houses. I watch them. They are getting brighter. Below me the enormous lava lake is rippling under a thousand dimmed lights. I look out across the glowing lake. A magnificent, lighted ship is anchored in the center of the lake. At last, I have seen a ship. My old childish dream has come true.

My Papa's voice is in my head: *Ships with white sails setting out for unknown seas.*

Where did he go? I think of his disappearing form walking into the forest. Did he manage to stumble his way back into Thornwold? Or was he lost in Brell's misty forest and killed by wild beasts as everyone thought? Surely, he was the rightful King of Thornwold and able to come and go between the worlds. Or perhaps he wasn't. *Your mother is waiting for me* he had said to me and had looked at me with unnaturally bright eyes. Whatever happened to him all those years ago, he was gone now.

The sound of music and laughter and people's dancing feet

rings from the ship's deck. Leaning on the balcony, I wish it were all a dream.

After the speech, Jack had stridden over to Ember and leaned over. He spoke in her ear forcefully before turning on his heel and coming over to me.

Bending over, he said, "Don't worry, Thea."

Then he was gone, but the steady assurance of these words and the warmth of his breath on my ear buzzed in a way I found comforting. Ember got up and followed him, still not looking in my direction. She appeared unhappy. I felt a twinge of satisfaction the announcement obviously hadn't gone her way.

"Eat, Thea, eat," Will said worriedly, pushing a plate of food at me. I was hungry but couldn't manage to work my knife and fork properly.

Iron was rubbing his head on my wrist. I picked him up and put him on my shoulder.

"It's all right, Thea," he said immediately when he was near my ear, "This wasn't part of the plan —" He stopped, realizing he had said the wrong thing.

I was staring straight ahead, trying to keep my face blank.

"What plan? I muttered.

"I can't tell you more because I don't know it all myself," he explained. His voice was genuinely upset. I knew it wasn't his fault, but I had begun to distrust everyone around me.

I took a sip of ice water and pushed some food around on the plate with my fork. "I'm not here to reclaim a throne." I said even more quietly. "I don't know what I'm doing here, but it isn't that."

"It wasn't right of Ember. She should have told you first. She should have let you decide."

"Decide nothing!"

This time I spoke loudly enough for the few people nearest me to hear and turn their heads curiously in my direction.

"Shhh, shhh —" said Will Waters. "Let's get her out of here, Iron."

"Yes, yes! Thea, please."

He was right. I didn't want to make a scene. I was at the mercy of these people and wasn't sure how they would take to their hero loudly protesting she wasn't going to do a damn thing for them after all.

No one paid attention as I rose and followed Will out of the room and down a long side passage. We took a few turns and went up a short flight of steps. At the top was a heavy door.

"Here we are," said Will trying to sound cheerful. "You can rest here. We can have some food sent to us."

I went inside and found myself in a small room. It was a bedroom and a sitting room combined. Gauzy, silken curtains hung around the low bed set against the wall. Across the room, were two comfortable looking high-backed chairs drawn up beside a small fire.

A polished wooden table with tea things on it sat between them. Steam issued from the kettle and the rich scent of something hot and sugary rose from the covered dish.

"Well!" exclaimed Will, "It looks like we are expected!" He bustled about, removing the covered dishes revealing hot scones and sticky pastries.

He led me to a chair and pushed at me until I sat down in it. I lifted Iron down from my shoulder to balance on one of the chair's thick arms and managed to pour myself some tea. The rich, raspberry scent reminded me of Abigail.

I felt tears sting my eyes and angrily wiped them away. I would give anything to be back in her cottage right now, fumbling to be her apprentice.

"I'm sorry Thea," said a soft voice, as if I had said my thoughts aloud.

I turned, startled, and saw Ember sitting in a shadowy corner farthest from the fire. I didn't know how I had missed her before. Her luminous skin glowed softly in the dark.

I jumped to my feet, knocking Ironsides to the seat of the chair. I strode over and stood in front of her.

"How could you?" I spat. "I am here to reclaim a throne, am I? Says who? You?"

She said nothing.

I didn't stop. "Is that why you were so dismayed my parents stayed in Brell? They wouldn't come back here and fight your

61

battle for you? So now you want their daughter to do it? Well, I won't. You can't make me."

Ember still didn't say anything. I gave up and walked away, picking up Iron, who lay on his back where he had landed, his feet wriggling. I threw myself into the chair.

"Sorry, Iron." I said and picked up my teacup with shaking hands.

Will giggled and Ironsides glared at him.

Ember cleared her throat. "As I said, I'm sorry, Thea. Jack was right. I should have spoken to you first."

"Yes, you should have," said Iron angrily, surprising me. "And you should have spoken to me. You should have told me what you were planning. I am still a member of the Council, am I not? Or does the Council even exist anymore?"

Ember was pained. "Of course you are, Iron. Of course it exists. I thought if Thea saw how much the people have loved and longed for her, she might feel differently."

She was looking at me pleadingly and I hated it, but I was sorry for her. My hunger was biting my insides. I took a scone covered in raspberry jam and clotted cream and bit into it. It tasted wonderful

Ember was relieved I wasn't going to yell at her again. "I should have told you everything, Thea," she repeated, "And you too, Iron." She looked at the turtle, who gave a full body hop that was the turtle equivalent of a shrug and drew his head halfway back in his shell.

"Well, tell me now," I said quietly. "Let's get this over with."

"What do you want to know?"

"Let's start with the stranger on the road. Who is he? I'm assuming you know about it?

Ember gave a guilty motion.

I rolled my eyes and glared at her.

"His name is Malius" Iron answered. "He's the ruler of Thornwold."

"Malius." I said and felt the name like salt on my tongue. It stung.

"Who is he?" I said again.

Ember closed her eyes and took a deep breath.

"Let me tell you the story from the beginning," she said. "I think you will find it answers many of your questions."

EMBER'S TALE

"Long Ago, there lived in the land of Thornwold a powerful family. The members of this family were handsome, strong, and unusually intelligent. They rose to wealth and power through intrigue, clever deals, and a particular strength of mind and purpose. Stoneham was their home.

For a while, all went well, but the family's power soon turned to corruption and cruelty. The people were stripped of their rights, taxed heavily to feed the pockets of the family who ruled over them, and if they couldn't pay, their lands were seized, and their children enslaved. The land had fallen into darkness.

Hope came in the form of an ordinary man. He was a good man. A soldier returned home from a far-off war in a distant land. He was a natural leader of the people. He was not young, but he was not old either, and he gathered an army of rebels and made plans to rise up to throw down the cruel family. His name was Anwar, meaning fire, and he would go on to restore the rights of the people and become the King of Thornwold." Ember paused. "He was helped in this task by Broon."

"Who is Broon?" I break in, my mouth full of pastry.

"How do I explain Broon?" mused Ember, looking at Ironsides. "He is Broon. He is the Thorn. The heart of the forest of Thornwold from which the land gets its power. He is at the center of it. Without it, he would die. Without him, the forest and all its creatures would die."

"But is he a man?" I asked in a puzzled voice.

"He is and he is not," answered Ember. "He looks like a man, if that is what you mean."

It wasn't what I meant, but I bit back my questions and listened as Ember went on.

"This man Anwar, he drove out the cruel family and banished them across the sea. They were outcast. Their resentment grew, fed by stories of Thornwold's prosperity and Anwar's successes. Reminders of what they had once had.

Meanwhile, Anwar was crowned King. He married and had

63

children, and his children grew up and married and had children of their own. Thornwold had a streak of luck with this family. Each ruler, always the eldest child, was just and sensible, and let themselves be guided by councils of wise men and women. For centuries there was peace. During this line of men, there came to them a gift. A glass Globe which granted the family the ability to see magic."

For a moment I don't comprehend, but Ember smiles at me, and I give a gasp.

"Yes, Thea. You have the power of seeing magic, and therefore controlling it easily. It came into your family, and they possessed this Globe for many years, using it wisely. They became the most powerful family in Thornwold. It was always kept a great secret, locked away in a vault under Stoneham and guarded closely."

"I've always said it was seeing colors," I said lamely. "The colors match what people feel. Are people's emotions magical? Are all people magical?"

Ember was pensive. "In a manner of speaking, yes. At least, people's strong emotions can create a type of magic. That sort of magic can't always be manipulated, of course," she explained. "But it can be used."

Ember paused while I tried to wrap my head around this and made herself a cup of tea. Ironsides shifted uncomfortably. He was lost in thought.

"The year your father was crowned king of Thornwold, miles away, far across the sea, a young man named Malius had spent his impoverished life listening to stories about the downfall of his prominent and powerful family. He was taught to resent the children of Anwar, the people of Thornwold, and to covet Stoneham.

As he grew, so did the burning in his heart for power and revenge. Promising his family he would retake Thornwold and regain the family honor, he set out for Thornwold in secret and soon came to the Dark Mountains. It was there, among the monks of the Dark Mountains, he learned a valuable secret.

"Dark Monks?" I ask. "Like dark magic?"

Ember shakes her head. "Magic can be used for both evil and good. But one cannot exist without the other to balance it. Good and evil is the user's intent, and not the magic itself. The Dark

Mountain Monks are scholars. Don't let their name make you believe they are evil. They are not. They are wise. They have studied magic and are now the self-appointed keepers of many ancient magical secrets. In part, to keep their knowledge, they have taken strict vows of silence.

It must have taken Malius a long time to find any information about a magical Globe and his own ties to it. This mysterious ancient tool had been lost centuries before in the Great War. It was this loss leading chiefly to his family's downfall.

You see, the Globe had been the property of Malius's ancient family, and the reason for all their wealth and power. It had been lost or stolen when Anwar defeated them and took Stoneham, and for many years, people who knew of it thought it was destroyed. By some odd twist of fate, it ended up falling into the hands of your family, Thea. Perhaps it has always meant to be part of Stoneham and is tied to the roots of the castle itself."

"And Malius stole it?"

"Malius must have found a reference to the location in his studies among the Dark Monks magical archives," agreed Ember, "Because he came to Stoneham."

"And found it?" I asked again. "And stole it?"

"Not yet. He was clever. He passed himself off as a young scholar eager to serve the royal family. He pleased King Douglas and the court with his knowledge and his charming manner. Broon and I did not trust him."

"Nor did I," Ironsides put in bitterly.

I looked at my turtle with wonder. "How old are you, Iron?" I demanded, but he only winked one of his eyes at me slowly.

Ember was looking upset. "I wish we had been more open with our misgivings," She said. "But we weren't. How could we know?"

"One day, Cecilia woke to find her ability to see magic gone. She knew that something had happened to the Globe. It quickly became apparent what had happened when Malius showed up, the servants behind him staring ahead blankly and moving only when Malius gave an order. The King and Queen were arrested and taken to the dungeons. Along with their infant daughter."

I stared at her, unable to speak. I had assumed I was born in Brell.

Ember smiled at me. "You were only two years old, Thea. You retained your magical ability."

"But how?" I asked. "If the Globe was now Malius's?"

"No one knows," Ember is thoughtful. "We've had many theories over the years, but Malius was unable to take your magic."

I am silent, thinking this over.

"Broon and I rescued you all, getting away through the secret passages under Stoneham. We got away into the forest with a few of your Mother's ladies and some older men-at-arms. We hid your parents away in my underground kingdom, but word must have come to Malius they were here.

When his soldiers, bewitched men who had been loyal soldiers of your Father's, were marching on the great plain separating Stoneham from the Forest of Thornwold, Broon and I brought our magic together. His earth and my fire shook the world and the plain fell in – and our enemies with it."

I can see it. The great rumble, fire in the sky, and the clouds rising for miles as screaming men fell into a bottomless pit. I shuddered.

It was as if she knew what I had seen in my mind.

"Broon was sorry to do it," Ember said, "Some of those men had been your Father's friends."

"Go on. Where does Brell come in?"

"With Stoneham on one side of an impassable chasm, and the forest and the caverns on the other, we felt safer, but we knew it was only a matter of time. The Mudglucks made the chasm a maze. They carved out the rock so there were thousands of dead ends. There is no easy way through it. It is impossible to find one's way from one side to the other without a guide. Still, Malius' soldiers find a way. We have even had them find my underground entrance."

I tried not to appear alarmed. Ember didn't notice.

"We decided your family must leave Thornwold as soon as they could. Going over the sea was not possible. It lies beyond Stoneham in the other direction. We felt it would be safer for you all to be hidden away in some ordinary place. A place where you might not draw attention.

Broon created a passage between Brell and the Thorn and your family went there. Ironsides went with them as protector. You have all been there for many years.

When you were about nine years old, your Father sent us word of his formal abdication. It came as a shock. He and your Mother had decided to not return, but perhaps they were happy in Brell. Broon sent him a letter, I believe, but – we had word of your Mother's death, and not long after, your Father's disappearance –" She stopped.

I didn't want to think about Mama's death or Papa's disappearance.

Instead I asked, "And Malius couldn't find them there?"

Ember spoke slowly. "Brell is an in-between place. It is always in the mist. It hides itself well, even from your world at times. For years, the forest has been impassable in that particular part of the forest, and of course, nearly every year since, Broon and I cast many confusion spells at the perimeter to shift any unwanted attention away from the area."

"The strange noises?" I asked, thinking of the dark shapeless forms swooping and thumping against the cottage. "Were those you?"

"Not all of them, no." said Ember. "Some of the noises were part of our spells, but many were from something else."

Her 'something else' made me shudder.

"I heard all of them," I said. "Once I heard my name."

"Your name?" asked Ember, alarmed. "Are you sure?"

"Yes. I heard someone calling me, and it woke me up."

"Perhaps you dreamt it," said Ember, but her voice didn't sound certain.

We sat for a while in silence. Will was asleep or pretending to be. Iron's head was half inside his shell. I hugged my knees tightly to me in front of the fire and thought it all over. Despite the warmth, I felt cold. The quiet was broken only by the crackle of flame and the pop of dry wood. No one was willing to speak.

"What happens now?" I said finally.

Ember looked at Ironsides. He looked back at her, sullenly.

"Well," said Ember, "you have the ability to see magic. For

now, I would like you to stay here with us. I can train you in the use of it."

"I mean about Malius," I said. "What's he after?"

"Exactly. What is he showing up in Brell for? I thought Brell was closed to him."

I am grateful to find Ironsides is my ally in this. He is as upset and confused as I am.

Ember was flustered. "Malius knows the Globe's magic left your parents but didn't leave you."

My heart is hammering against my ribcage, thundering in my ears, as I realized what her words meant.

"You mean he doesn't like the idea?"

Ember didn't answer.

Iron was angry. "Why can't he be satisfied with taking Stoneham and the Globe? Why does it matter if Thea still has her ability?"

Ember gazed at me. "Because she is a formidable enemy to him. Her power matches his. She has the ability to become the greatest sorceress in the world if she likes. She can see magic, as he does, and so she is a threat."

"But I'm not. I don't even want this magic!"

As I said it, I wasn't sure if it were true. I had always been able to see colors glowing from people. What would my world be like if I couldn't see those swirling colors?

I pictured myself skillfully moving the colors this way and that. I wondered what the possibilities were if I learned how.

My thought must have shown on my face. Ember took my hands and sat down in front of me. "Thea, I can help you learn to control your abilities, but it is great danger you walk into and you may not return. You must know everything. I must tell you about the Globe."

"I never said I was walking into anywhere," I snapped, shaking her off. "You had no right to tell the people I would. If I don't do this, it's on you to explain to them why."

I stopped. I had said "if" and we both knew it.

"What about the Globe?" I muttered.

"The Globe is powerful and has many secrets. It can be used to control others. To create others."

"So Malius uses it to control everyone in Stoneham?"

"It's more. It can be used to make inanimate objects live and move. He has built an army out of nothing. Soldiers who never tire and never thirst. They are constantly making their way through the chasm and into the forest and we have to be vigilant in our defense. As you might imagine, it's a full-time job." She said this last wearily.

"And they wounded Jack?" asked Iron. "Is that where Broon has been?"

"When Thea arrived here, Malius got wind of it, and sent his soldiers out to track her down."

I had been followed. I shuddered as I thought about my long journey through the forest. All the while not knowing I had an indestructible army behind me.

"How did he find Brell?" asked Iron.

Ember shook her head. "We don't know exactly. Perhaps he followed Broon and I. Traces of our magic lingers near the border. It was only a matter of time before he was going to spot it."

"I can't go back." I said.

Iron and Ember looked at me.

"I can't go back without leading him or this army straight to Abigail or Bol or –" I stop, panicked.

"Are they safe? Maggie and Thomas?" I insisted. "Tell me they are safe."

Ember looked uncertain but determined to be honest.

"I don't know, Thea."

I buried my face in my hands and moaned.

Iron rubbed his head on my arm. "He's not after them, Thea. He knows you are here. He might leave Brell alone."

I was slightly comforted by this. "What am I to do? I can't go back. I can't stay here. My parents couldn't stay here either. You said so."

"This is where the plan comes in." said Ember, "We've been working on it for many years. When your Father and Mother decided not to return, I admit, we were flustered. All the visions had shown us Cecilia of Thornwold returning and taking back the throne, and we had assumed it was her we saw in the visions. But visions are funny things and aren't always accurate."

She gazed into my face intently. "But honestly, Thea, you do look so much like her. The same red hair. So pretty."

I brushed this aside impatiently, noting how she hasn't mentioned my Papa. Only my Mama.

"So now you think it's my responsibility? Because of a vision that may not even be right?" My voice is high and accusing.

"We can only hope it is right." Ember said. "You are the heir and it's been twenty years. Malius's power grows. We can't hold out much longer against him."

I was silent. Iron said, "What is it you expect her to do?"

Ember smiled. "The Globe must be destroyed. It is the source of his power. Afterward, he can be killed."

"And how am I to do this?" I demanded.

"That," Ember explained, "Is what the plan is all about."

The Plan

I stand on the balcony, listening to the music on the ship, and think over the whole story I had heard. I still wasn't promising anything, I told myself. Ember had told me I would hear all about the plan in the morning and she had left me alone with Iron and Will. I had finally gone to bed, exhausted, Iron's shell bumping my head on the pillow.

Now I found I couldn't sleep. I rub my head tiredly and find a loose twig, stuck in my braid. My hair is filthy.

There comes a soft creak from behind me. A small door I hadn't noticed before swings slightly open. I am alarmed, but go over to it, pushing it open.

Inside is a small room with a bathtub. Steaming scented water rises from the tub, and towels are placed next to it. I look all around me, expecting to see a maid, but no one is there. The house has anticipated my wants and answered them. An oval mirror, rimmed in gold, stands next to a small chair, where clean clothes have been laid out for me.

I strip and wash off the dirt and grime accumulated on my skin and hair. How long since I had left Brell? A day? Two? I am not sure how much time has passed.

I spend a long time in the bath. The scented water smells of honeysuckle. The golden charm is still around my neck. I wash it clean in the soapy water and look at it carefully. The lavender tinted glass letter sparkles, and the flower carvings are clearer now. 'S' for Stoneham, I think. The chain buzzes on my neck, telling me I'm right. There's one mystery solved.

When I am clean enough, I put on the soft underclothes and

71

the dress left for me on the back of the chair. I am pleased to find it fits easily and isn't too long. The bodice is fitted without being laced. The skirt l layered without being heavy. The soft green slippers are much more comfortable than my old shabby boots, which have been left in the main room.

I comb and dry my hair as well as I can, leaving it loose. It falls nearly to my waist. I examine myself in the oval mirror. I am different, older. The clothes make me look like someone important.

"Princess Thea," I whisper aloud, trying to picture a crown on my head. I can't.

I wander back into the main room. Iron is still asleep on my pillow. I glance around for Will, but don't see him. He must have woken and left in the night. Perhaps he has a house of his own. A family.

I open the French doors and go out on the balcony. The lake is still and there is no sign of anyone. The ship has finally gone quiet. It is fully daylight now, though early. There are a few men I take to be gardeners, walking below with spades and buckets.

The gardens are beautiful. Set among brilliant greenery, winding mazes make interesting patterns. Blossoming flowers and clusters of glowing gems intermingle to create dazzling displays. Fountains of cool water sparkle in the light from the high stone ceiling.

The golden fallout dust of leftover magic is everywhere. It settles on the balcony balustrade and on my newly washed hair and skin. I sneeze, then laugh. Maybe I'm allergic, like Iron. I turn away from this beautiful sight, as the turtle's head emerges from his shell at last.

He yawns and eyes me. "You look much better, Thea."

"Thanks," I say, looking down at the dress. "It's nice, isn't it?"

"Mm," says the turtle absently. "Has there been any breakfast?"

There is the sound of the rattle of dishes. I go over to the small table and find the tea things of last night gone. In their place are new dishes revealing bacon, eggs, and toast. Hot coffee, cold cream, and lumps of sugar are next to these. For Ironsides there is some fresh fruit and water.

He has made his way over and I put a dish of strawberries and melon down in front of him. I pour myself some coffee and add a little sugar to it.

"I could get used to this," I remark, helping myself to eggs and toast. "Does anything you want just appear?"

"Not anything. The basic necessities. Food. Clothes. Fire for warmth. Those kinds of thing." Iron is dismissive.

"Is it magic all over Thornwold, or only here?"

"Oh, there's magic everywhere, but this is Ember's house," Iron explains through mouthfuls of strawberry. "In the rest of Thornwold, the citizens are similar to Brell's, except not horrible."

"Did you think Brell people were horrible?" I ask, amused.

"Well, not some of them. Maggie and Bol are fine. Abigail is all right. Thomas is a bit loud at times. But the rest of them." Ironsides shudders.

I laugh at this. We eat in silence. I am finishing my second cup of coffee when the door to my room shakes with a sharp knock. I go over and open it. Jack is standing there.

"Good morning. I wasn't sure you'd be up."

"I woke up a little while ago."

He is dressed more simply he was last night, in a loose shirt and comfortable trousers. He wears black boots. His dark hair falls forward. It makes me want to push it out of his eyes. Those eyes sweep over me approvingly and I am even more awkward.

I open the door wider and gesture at the table. "Would you like breakfast?"

Iron is still munching his way through a melon and he pauses, glaring at Jack as if daring him to take it away.

Jack shakes his head. "No thank you. I'm sent to bring you and Ironsides to the Council."

"Now?" asks Iron, swallowing. "They don't waste much time."

Jack is annoyed, but his voice is polite. "Broon has arrived, you see. He wishes to meet Thea, and to see you, of course, sir."

Iron appears mollified by this. He takes one last bite and I go over to him, scooping him up. He perches on my shoulder.

We leave my room and walk down the long hallway. I gaze around me. The ceiling is made of colored glass. It makes colorful designs on the marble floor. The wide hall leads one way to last night's banquet room, now swept clean of all signs of feasting. We go the other direction. Long windows facing the gardens line this hall, and the brilliant 'morning" light streams through them.

"Are you well-rested?"

"Yes, thank you."

"How old are you?"

Jack is looking at me a trifle arrogantly. I am defensive.

"Sixteen. How old are you?"

Again, the deep, rich gray green is swirling out of him. I understand it is magic I'm seeing, and I move away from him in response, but his quiet apology is sincere.

"Sorry. You look incredibly young for what they would have you do."

"And what is that?"

"You'll find out soon enough."

I open my mouth to argue, but Ironsides says in a soothing tone, "The Council will tell us their plan."

I reflect that the turtle's mood has been improved by sleep and food. He leans forward on my shoulder.

"Who does the Council consist of these days, Jack?"

"Broon, Ember, me, Dominus, and there's been a special inclusion of Will."

Iron frowns. "That's all? No one else? Serafin? Antignon? Not even Flavius?"

"Dead," says Jack. His tone is cold.

There is silence.

"I'm sorry, Jack."

Ironsides speaks to Jack kindly. I look at both of them in surprise. A flash of deep grief crosses Jack's face, but he turns his head away.

We have reached a door made of some material I can't identify. It isn't stone. It is different than iron, lighter in color. On it, animals and birds are carved. From a smooth grove of trees, a deer leaps, frozen in mid-air, startling a rabbit from a circle of ferns. The lines of it glimmer with their own light. As Jack puts his hand to it, the door swings open.

The room we enter is dark. I can make out a large wooden table with soft velvet chairs around it. A fire glows at one end of the room in a massive fireplace. Tapestries cover the marble walls, deep red woven with golden figures and scenes. Rich, velvet curtains cover long windows, blocking out light. Above us swings a chandelier, lit with dozens of candles. It casts a dim light around the room.

"At last," Ember rises from her chair. "Please come in and be seated."

As we step inside the room, the door swings shut behind us. Jack goes off into a corner and throws himself down on a brown settee. The faces turn toward me eagerly and I stand still.

A huge man, looking out of place in the enclosed room, rises and walks toward us. He is clothed in soft material that ripples over his arms and chest. His legs are covered in the same, but of a darker hue. A large deep green cloak hangs from his shoulders, fastened with bronze fasteners. His brown boots are enormous and well-worn.

He kneels in front of me, his dark eyes staring into mine, studying my face. I am unable to look away. He turns to Ironsides and smiles, white teeth in a dark face.

The copper waves coming off him are beautiful and I blink back tears. His glowing color is mixed with small sparks and streaks of swirling golden light. It doesn't disappear, but curves around the three of us in ribbons. I am reminded of my Papa, of Maggie and Thomas, and of Abigail looking at me when she thought I didn't see.

"Hello, Ironsides," he says to the turtle on my shoulder. "Well met, old friend."

Iron appears nonchalant, but there is joy in his voice. "Hello, Broon. It's good to see you again."

The giant man turns his eyes on me. "Thea." He only says my name, but it rings, a clear bell in the silent room.

This is Broon. His eyes look into me, ferreting out the things I keep hidden. I don't mind. It's as if we are old, dear friends. There is the noise of water, songbirds, and the sparkle of sunlight on a rippling brook. I know what everyone means now. Broon isn't a man, and what he is, there is no name for. Satisfied with what he finds, he smiles at me, "Welcome home."

"Thank you," I whisper.

He leads me to the table, courteously pulling a chair out for me. I sit down. Will sits next to me, pleased to be included. Broon sits across from me. Ember stands near the head of the table, even though there are four other empty chairs and one plushy footstool.

75

Three of the chairs are for the people Iron and Jack had mentioned. These will remain empty.

"Where is Dominus?" asks Ember, placing her hands on the shining surface of the table.

"Late asss usual," comes a hissing voice, and an enormous, brilliantly colored snake comes drifting across the floor from behind one of the curtains.

I draw back in horror. His patterned skin is spotted with splashes of red and gold, crisscrossed by faint white scars. His emerald eyes glow in the firelight as he coils his body up onto the footstool next to me.

"My apologiesss," he bobs his giant head to me and flicks his long tongue at the turtle on my shoulder, who grips me with his claws.

"Hello Ironsssidesss," the snake's voice is lazy and amused. "Welcome back."

"Hello, Dominus," the turtle is nervous, and I move the shoulder holding him away from where the snake sits. Dominus curves his mouth upwards in a smile and shakes his head.

"No need to fear, princesss, Ironsssidesss and I are old friendsss."

"Of a sort," says Iron stiffly.

Broon's booming laugh makes everybody jump. "Come, come, everyone! Iron, Dominus isn't going to eat you. Dominus, stop teasing him! Thea, Dominus appears more frightening than he is."

"Dominus, behave yourself," admonishes Ember.

Dominus turns his head on one side, "Of courssse," There is still amusement in his voice, and he winks one of his emerald eyes at me. I let out a breath. I decide I might like him once I get used to him.

"Let's begin, shall we?" asks Ember, looking around at each one of us. She smiles at me in a reassuring way, but I don't smile back.

"As we all know, Althea Persis Elizabeth Cecilia Morgan is the rightful heir to the throne of Stoneham and the land of Thornwold. She is the one we have seen in visions."

"How can you be sure?" Ironsides says in a grumpy tone.

Ember regards him. "We can't be sure, but, nevertheless, she is the rightful ruler of Thornwold according to the law. She has the Globe's magic. It's been twenty years since Malius took the throne. All of this was in the vision."

Broon clears his throat. "Visions are not always correct, it's true, Iron, and there are a few discrepancies if we are being honest."

"What discrepancies?" I say, finding my voice.

"We had foreseen Cecilia being the one to come back and reclaim the throne, for one. But we could have been mistaken in our assumptions. You are so like your mother."

I grimace. I note again how they don't mention my Papa. They must have known about his death, and no one wanted to refer to it. I swallow something.

"Is that it?" asks Iron.

"We had foreseen Brell being important, being significant to the fight we have before us," says Ember. "It might still be so. We aren't sure."

"What else?"

We all jump as Jack speaks for the first time. I had forgotten he was there.

Broon gazes at Jack. "We have had a vision of Malius being killed by his own son."

I open my eyes wide. "You didn't say he had a son!"

Ember is uncomfortable, "I wasn't sure it was necessary."

"But where – "I say, when Iron interrupts me.

"Thea is the one in the vision to get the Globe and destroy it, is that what you mean?"

"Our plan does not include killing Malius. If that's what *you* mean." Ember answers him.

Relief sweeps over me in a wave. I am certain I could never kill anyone.

"But we are sure the Globe, being used as it was by Malius for so many years, must contain all of Malius' power and life force." Ember continues, "If it is destroyed, it stands to reason he will die too."

My spirits sink as quickly as they had risen, "But won't it destroy me, too? It will take away my magic, won't it?"

"Your powers appear to be separate from the Globe's influence," comes Broon's calm voice, "You have not spent your life using it and putting all of your energy into it. It's destruction shouldn't hurt you."

I am not so certain, but I am willing to let it pass for now.

"So all Thea has to do is sneak into Thornwold and smash it?" demands Jack. His voice is angry, and I don't think it's from any gallantry on my behalf. "How does she do this? She isn't even able to control her own magic."

I flush and glare at him. How does he know so much about me?

"I can learn! I'm smart, you know. I nearly went to Moor's famous university."

Jack only snorts. *He doesn't even know what a university is* I think.

"Children," Broon admonishes us, "Peace."

He turns to Ember. "How long will it take to teach her?"

"Not long. A month perhaps."

I swallow. A month! I have to set out to find a magic Globe in a castle, evade a magical army hunting me down, and face an evil ruler who wants me dead? Using only what magical skills I can learn in a month?

"No," I say. My voice echoes through the room. "I can't do it." I turn to Broon. "You know I can't. I know you've seen me. I can't even make a healing potion."

The others in the room look puzzled, and Broon opens his mouth to speak, but Iron interrupts, "Now hold on. Just hold on, Thea. Let's get it all out. What exactly is the plan?"

Looking relieved, Ember unrolls a large map on the table. We all crane forward to look. The building plans of a castle, with markings and notations on it etched in silver, lay in front of us. Hundreds of squares and rectangles and circles represent rooms and towers. A long tangle of smaller rectangles connect underneath these creating a maze. These have been highlighted with bright blue markings and notes.

"Here is the map of Stoneham. We spent many years gathering all of the information you see here. It shows all the secret entrances and exits which run beneath the stone floors.

The plan is to train Thea to use her magical ability. She must learn to defend herself and protect herself. She must learn to find her way in the dark. We can't be certain how much Malius knows about these underground spaces, but we assume it is well-guarded and magically protected."

"Thea will have to travel through the Thorn, led by Jack and company," Broon puts in with a nod to Dominus and Will. "And through the chasm. Once she has made her way to the edge of Stoneham, we can help her by creating a distraction, while she finds her way inside, through the tunnels, and to the Globe."

"I know all the ways into Stoneham very well, your Highnesssss," hisses Dominus.

"And I helped create the mazes in the chasm," says Will, "I know the quickest way through!"

There is no mention of getting me out of the castle and back home.

"What kind of distraction?" asks Ironsides, his voice suspicious.

"A war," Jack is exhilarated. "We're going to start a war!"

I snort. Everyone turns to stare at me, except Ironsides, who smugly clears his throat and Jack, who scowls.

Disconcerted but determined, I say, "Surely this is the oldest trick in the book? Malius knows I'm here. He'll be expecting something like that. Draw out the armies? Create chaos? It's as ancient a trick as the Trojan Horse itself."

"What's a Trojan?" Will whispers, but everyone ignores him. For a moment no one speaks.

"Excellent!" laughs Ember. "You will make a thoughtful and strategic ruler of Thornwold. Yes, Thea, we've thought of that. It's why we are going to create an illusion."

Broon is nodding at me in approval. "Except for one difference. In the Trojan Horse, there was no magic. Not that we know of anyway. But the Thorn is full of it. There's going to be a second you, leading the army."

I am not surprised Broon knows the story of the Trojan Horse. "But how?"

"Magic," says Ironsides. "A doppelganger."

"Not real, of course," says Ember, "Merely a tracing in the air. Our hope is by the time you have destroyed the Globe, it will be too late for Malius."

Again, there is no mention of what happens to me after Malius realizes someone has infiltrated his castle and is trying to steal and destroy his magic. I have my doubts about the idea of this 'tracing' but decide it's best to leave it for now.

"But how —" I say again, but Ember has anticipated my question.

"I am going to teach you how," she says in a tone reminding me of Abigail, "I am going to teach you everything you need to know." My heart sinks as I think of the hole blown in Abigail's cottage wall.

Ironsides has gained confidence. "After the teaching is finished, where does Thea go from here and how does she get there?"

"The first stop is Lilywell."

"What?" I ask.

"My house," says Broon. "It is called Lilywell. It is a safe place and deep in the Thorn. Jack?"

Jack stands up. "We'll go by the Old Road."

Dominus nods, but Will gasps. "The Old Road," his voice trembles, "Surely not?"

"The Old Road is safe," Jack says confidently. I can understand why he is a soldier. "No one uses it anymore. It hasn't attracted much attention over the years."

"But the Watchers?" says Will, still sounding fearful.

"They won't harm us," insists Jack. "Many of them are asleep, aren't they, Broon?"

Broon's expression is odd. "Asleep," he says in his deep, musical voice, "Or perhaps merely waiting?"

I blink. The copper flowing off Broon is changing to a color I have never seen. It's so rich and warm, I could fall into it. There are music and voices in the distance. The sound fills me up. I sway forward in my chair.

Iron digs his claw into my shoulder. I sit up, realizing my eyes had closed. As the color fades, so does the sound. I am embarrassed, but Broon only nods at me, a knowing look on his face.

"Broon!" the turtle says loudly, "Are the Watchers any danger to us?"

Broon shifts his gaze to the turtle in surprise, as if remembering where he is. "No, Iron. But they are not bound by the same laws. They owe their loyalty only to Thornwold."

He looks back at me and his face is thoughtful. "They may recognize a true heir of Thornwold. I guess we'll see."

"So we risk being seen or caught if we travel the Old Road?" Iron is determined to ignore Broon's musings.

"Perhaps," says Ember. "But you risk it on any path you take from here."

"I think we need to have someone else along." Iron looks at Broon, but Broon shakes his head.

"I have business many leagues from here."

"Where?" asks the turtle, his voice sharp.

Unlike the others, Ironsides does not regard Broon with the same awe and respect they do. Broon, instead of being angry or annoyed by this, seems to enjoy it.

"I will appeal to the Light Mountain people, the Plainspeople of Glasshedge, and the Seafolk, of course."

He pauses. "And the Monks of Dark Mountain."

This startles everyone except me.

"Who are the Dark Monks?" I say, but no one answers me.

"They won't help us, and you know it," says the turtle, his voice flat.

"They won't help Malius either," counters Broon. "The Monks are their own people, Ironsides, as you well know."

He emphasizes this last and everyone except Ember, looks from the giant man to the turtle.

"No need to go into all that," the Lady of Fire cuts in.

Dominus lifts his head. "I will be there, Ironsssidesss," he hisses in a way that is meant to be reassuring, "I am sssstrong and ussseful." His silvery tongue glints in the firelight.

Ironsides closes his eyes.

Will sits up, bouncing his seat. "Don't forget me!" he says. He reminds me of a rather dirty, but likable, younger brother. Jack and I both grin at him and are confused to find ourselves in agreement on something.

"As long as you can follow orders," says Iron. Will winks at me.

"I'm going too," Jack puts in.

I am less pleased by this but try not to show it. Animosity creeps from Jack toward me and I am uncertain why. I plan to ask Ember about it.

"Good," agrees Ember. "You'll leave here and make your way to Lilywell. From there you'll follow a map through the chasm."

Will protests, but Ember holds up her hand, silencing him. "Yes, I know you know the way without any maps, Will, but you

81

must follow the track we've laid out for you. We have a special route. It will take you right to the walls of Stoneham. At the end of this path is a stair. You must make your way up it to the entrance we've marked here." She points at the map to a small silver star.

"Simple enough," says Jack, sounding confident. "When will she be ready to leave?"

"When I am sure she is ready," says Ember, but Broon shakes his head.

"It won't do. Malius is already preparing. He is sending soldiers through the chasm and into the Thorn nearly every day, hunting for her. We can't afford to wait too long."

"But you have been able to divert them so far?" asks Iron.

"I've done what I can as far as protection goes." Broon turns to me. "Thea, you must learn quickly. Do you understand? Your past is past. This is a different kind of magic. And a different kind of study. You were born with it, which helps, but it takes years to master the Globe's magic. We don't have years. Days only. A week at best. You must learn all you can. Don't worry about what you haven't been able to do. Focus on what you can do."

He has seen my fumbled attempts in Abigail's cottage, I'm sure of it. How he has seen it, I can't say. It is the first of many mysterious things about Broon I will never understand.

"I can teach you enough in a week." Ember looks at Broon for approval.

"A week," he agrees.

Only Iron and I glance at each other. A week is so short. Seven days.

The Council adjourns and we head out into the soft glow of the marble, magical house. I hesitate behind the others. It occurs to me no one has asked me if I agree to any of it.

I hadn't once said I would go and destroy their Globe for them. Or I would unseat Malius and be their new ruler. Distracted by new information, I simply hadn't asked about other possibilities. Other options. Ironside nudges my ear in a worried way and I follow Ember toward the main hall.

Because there aren't any other options, I think. I can't go back to Brell and lead Malius there. I can't escape Brell or Thornwold and end up leading Malius somewhere else. I can't stay here and wait for him to come find me. I have no choice but to follow the plan that has been laid out for me since the day I was born. Since my Papa waived his birthright, effectively handing it to me.

For the first time, I am angry with him. He knew what he was passing on to me. He must have known someday Malius would find us.

But how could he? A small voice insists. He wanted to keep us ordinary. Keep us safe. He didn't know Mama would die and I would promise my future to Abigail. If only I had left Brell sooner. If only I hadn't promised Abigail to be her apprentice. If only I had followed my own inclinations and went to study at the university two years ago. Perhaps Malius wouldn't have found me. Perhaps none of this would be happening.

I have a wave of resignation so intense it makes me want to cry. I'm as trapped in Thornwold as I was in Brell.

The Old Road

One week later, the night is still and oppressive. I follow behind Ember along the dark path near the edge of the glowing lake. My red hair has been braided around my head and held in place by pins. A soft cloak covers my dark green tunic and swings to the edge of sturdy brown boots. In my pack I carry my Mama's gifts, extra clothes, and a container for water.

It has been one week since the Council meeting. I had spent seven days learning how to control the magic I could see.

I had learned to throw a Seeking, a searching spell that found traces of magic or physical presence. For this we enlisted Will to hide among the rocks in the garden while I sent the spell searching for him. He wasn't difficult to find because he always laughed, claiming the Seeking 'tickled' when it found him.

I learned to throw shafts of magic the color of blue flame and slice through rock. Once I got the hang of it, it was fun. I smashed boulders with a swift motion. I cut through cliffs with a quick flash of azure. All I had to do was channel my frustration or anger in the direction of the object and it was simple. I had plenty of anger and frustration.

I learned to open my mind to visions but was cautioned visions weren't always real. Once I opened my mind, it was difficult to close off. The faint pictures made no sense.

A still pool with water lilies, rings rippling to the banks, warm stone and glowing flowers reminding me of Abigail's cottage, a glimpse of tall mountains with the light of the fading sun touching their peaks, an old man with gray hair, who gazed out at me with vacant eyes. My head ached after such exertions and I felt sleepless.

I had the worst trouble with defensive and protection spells. Ember tried to teach me to cast a net of bright light around myself. This was a basic spell of protection. I wove it, concentrating on the pattern of weaving, but when Ember shot an attack at me, the net dissolved into nothing. When her fire had burned my arm for the seventh time, I sat down in despair and pain.

Ember came over and took my arm, soothing it with a few drops of silver from a vial. In seconds it had healed. She tucked the vial into my hand.

"You'll need this. You must remember to concentrate and clear your mind. You must focus your emotions. You are distracted. Think of how you channel your anger to throw magic and turn the power into a protection toward yourself."

But I didn't know how to do this, and I didn't know how to stop noticing other things. The golden leftover dust swirling around us, Jack's lean frame, rich gray-green energy seeping from him as he watched us. Most of all, the overwhelming sense of something that felt, for lack of a better word, awkward. The net of protection was too large for me to handle, and the light too bright. I couldn't focus it inward.

"It's difficult to hold onto it when someone is shooting fireballs at me," I snapped.

Ember said nothing, and I felt guilty. This was the reason we were here. Malius would shoot much worse things at me. I changed the subject.

"That night on the road," I ventured, "Malius could have killed me easily, but he didn't. Do you think it's strange?"

"He wasn't sure it was you, perhaps. Or, if he was sure, he may have felt more secure killing you in the forest and away from the village."

This was unsettling to hear. I didn't want to think about it. Instead I stood up and went and took my position again. Taking a deep breath, I began building the net of protection.

This time Malius was clear in my head, his eyes like mine, assessing me. The strange surge of color crawled toward me and I had an odd sensation in my fingertips. I opened my eyes.

"That's right," Ember's voice was joyful. "Concentrate. Focus."

The white net I was building grew larger. I held it around me, enlarging it, and moving it toward Ember while keeping it around myself. It was an extension of my hands. The sensation was the buzz of the chain of Mama's necklace around my neck.

"Good –" Ember said, as the strands of shining white wove around us.

I was still concentrating on the way Malius's strange magic whirled from him, when it dissolved, disappearing in darkness. I couldn't hold the net. It shattered even as I thought about it. The net went flying into nothingness and I dropped to the ground exhausted, but Ember was pleased.

"Very good, Thea!" She examined my face, smiling.

"But I dropped it. I lost concentration."

"We'll keep practicing."

On the last night, Ember and I sat by the fire in my small room. I took out the pouch of my Mama's gifts and showed her the necklace I wore. Hopeful, I watched her as she opened the scroll.

She read it, her lips moving soundlessly over the words.

"You can read it! What does it say?"

"It's a translation of an ancient story. About a man who plays his lyre in the underworld and leads his love out from the kingdom of death." The story sounded familiar, but I couldn't remember where I had heard it before.

I pointed to the flute. "Is that what this does? Brings people back from the dead?" I thought of Mama and Papa and felt a confused wave of excitement and fear.

Ember picked up the flute and examined the strange symbols on it, puzzled. "These markings are like none I've ever seen. It is a magical object, but you must not try to use it for something it isn't fit for." She handed it back to me. "It is against the laws of nature to bring the dead back to life. It is specifically against the laws of magic, as well."

I ignored this because I had thought of something else, "That night! I heard whistling in the trees when I 'crossed over' from Brell to Thornwold. Do you think it was an instrument? Could someone have been playing a flute?"

"I don't know, Thea. Perhaps. But it stands to reason what you heard was no more than a distraction to turn your feet from the path and towards Malius. From what you have told me, it sounds as if the Thorn itself rose up to rescue you."

I threw myself back against the chair in irritation. No one had answers for me. I pulled the necklace out of my collar and felt the familiar buzz against my skin.

I took it off and handed it to Ember. "What about this?"

Ember took the necklace and held it up in the firelight. "Beautiful."

"Yes, but what does it do?"

"Do?"

"Yes," I was frustrated now. "It buzzes on my skin. It has to be magical. So what does it do?"

"Nothing I imagine." She traced the lavender glass letter 'S' with a finger. A small bright spark glowed on her finger and she pulled away quickly, puzzled. I watched her face eagerly, but she only smiled and shook her head.

"It's magical to be sure, but it doesn't mean it does anything at all. It may be a charm of some kind. Something Cecilia made herself, by the look of it."

She leaned forward and put it gently back over my head. "If your mother made it and left it for you, Thea, perhaps it will keep you safe."

In the dark of the early morning, I try to remember this as I follow Ember out to a worn path beside the lake.

Dominus is nowhere to be seen, and Ironsides yawns on my shoulder. Somewhere in the shadows behind me, Will follows closely, sometimes a two-legged gnome, sometimes changing himself into earth and moving through the dry, sandy path.

To one side of us is the rough wall of the cavern disappearing into blackness above. The soft splash of the lava lake is the only sound besides Will's transformations, which are a rustling sound, wind moving through grass.

Ember slows her pace as we climb a slight hill. When we reach the top, she swerves abruptly and stops before a rocky outcrop in the wall.

"Here," she says and makes a slight gesture.

The protrusion in the wall shudders and widens, revealing an entrance into the side of the cavern. I peer inside to see a long, dimly lit passage running away from us until it twists around a corner and vanishes into gloom.

Ember bends forward and touches the air blowing out of the opening. She raises her head in satisfaction. "It appears to be undisturbed."

Will has come up out of the earth and stands, a half-formed gnome, at her feet. He tests the edge of the entrance with his hand. "Solid rock, no good."

Ember turns to me. I am shivering and not only from the cool morning air.

"There isn't much time, Thea. I must say farewell quickly. Trust your own instincts. Remember to focus." She takes me in her warm arms. I hug her back, blinking back tears.

From the dark path behind her a figure emerges and turns into Jack. He is dressed for travelling in a warm gray cloak and heavy pack balanced on his shoulder. A shabby scabbard and bright hilt are fastened to his side, crossing his chest with a brown leather strap.

"We're all here? No wait, where is the snake?" Iron has lifted his head from my shoulder. I look around but the red and gold reptile is not here.

Jack shrugs. "He is meeting us up above. Gone ahead to scout it out a bit."

"That's all right then," Iron gazes at Ember and his voice is unusually soft. "Goodbye for now."

The Lady of Fire smiles at the turtle. "It won't be for so long this time." She reaches out her hand and traces the gold on his shell briefly. Ironsides withdraws his head a little and hunches down.

I have a flash of something across my vision. A man is standing next to Ember. He wears a dark hood. He isn't young, and his face is worn and lined, but his beautiful dark eyes are humorous and bright.

I shake my head and blink and the image vanishes. I look at Ember in confusion, but she smiles at me with an imperceptible shake of her head. I consider my turtle.

Will is making impatient circles in the dust. "Let's go. The sooner we are off, the sooner we can reach Lilywell."

"Yes, you must be off now," agrees Ember. "I shouldn't keep this door open too long."

I turn and step inside the entrance. Will pops up out of the sandy ground and comes to stand beside me. Jack enters, running his hand along the looming walls. Ember moves back from the cliff.

As she does, the door closes, silently reshaping itself into the rough wall. My last glimpse of the cavern is Ember's beautiful face, sparkling in the soft light from the hanging Quickwillow homes.

The forest of Thornwold lays in a deep hush. The scent of spring earth drifts in the quiet air. Far away, a bird calls a sleepy note and is still. A small pool with a glassy surface reflects the perfect circle of trees and sky above it. It is broken by the large gray stone laying in its exact center. There is a sharp rustling noise and a drowsy looking wild rabbit hops out from the undergrowth. Stopping, he stretches his slim body and scratches one long ear with an even longer hind foot.

A loud crack splits the silence. The rabbit shrinks to the earth and is gone in flash of dull brown. In the center of the gleaming shallow pool the large rock has cracked in two. Waves ripple outward and run over the edges of the bank. A startled group of frogs, perched on a wet branch, vanish with a spattering of plop-plops.

Climbing out of the split rock, I squeeze myself up through the opening. I balance myself on my hands, wincing when the sharp edges of the stone press into my palms. Throwing one booted leg up on the slope of stone, I pull myself up even farther, only to lose my balance. I go tumbling into the water with a splash.

Ironsides, who has been sitting on my shoulder, goes sailing through the air and lands with a thud on the grass. He had pulled in his legs, and now, he puts them out and is annoyed to find himself lying upside down. He waves his short legs in fury, but to no avail. I sit up, sputtering.

Jack climbs out of the stone after me, and gazes at the scene before him in a bemused way. He swings up onto the rock and jumps to the bank without a drop of water touching him. He offers his hand to me, but I ignore it, struggling to my feet with a great deal of noise and splashing. He shrugs, turning away, and takes his heavy pack off with a sigh.

Will, emerging from the muddy bank, peers at me as I wring out my cloak and try to get the strands of wet hair out of my eyes. My braid has come lose.

"Shhh!" he says.

I clamber up the grassy bank to the level forest floor. I scowl at Will, but he has shrunk into a muddy lump with wide eyes. He vanishes into the earth, only to appear a moment later in the grass, looking himself again. He shakes himself and pounds one side of his head to get the sand out. It comes out in a fine stream of dust.

I find Ironsides and choke back a laugh, righting him. Without thanking me, he scurries to the edge of the pool and dives in, disappearing without a sound. I pull off my sodden cloak and spread it on some low bushes to dry.

My pack, which has escaped the worst of the pool, has extra clothes in it. I take it and start to walk away, looking for privacy.

"Don't go too far," calls Jack.

Defiant, I walk a little farther away. The surrounding shrubs are thicker here, and there is a convenient log to serve as a seat. I sit, pulling off my wet boots and emptying them. A dazed looking, slightly squished frog falls from one of the toes. I am shivering now. I change my wet stockings, tunic, and underthings for dry ones. Carrying my wet boots and clothes, I return to the others.

"Can we build a fire?" I ask Will, who is searching around the backs of trees and under stones. He shoves his nose into the undergrowth and startles the brown rabbit. It leaps across the clearing and disappears into a clump of bracken.

Will looks at Jack for approval.

"A smokeless fire," he cautions Will. With this he disappears into the forest.

Will pulls from his bag a handful of smooth black stones. I wring out my wet clothes and watch the Mudgluck lay the stones in a careful circle. He motions over them once, then twice. The rocks lay quivering and then glow a bright yellow. They begin to throw off heat. Jack's right. There is no visible smoke.

I arrange my wet clothes around the stones on some nearby bushes and rocks, draw in closer to the glowing circle, and hold my hands out to its radiating warmth. I am surprised at the intensity of the heat, and soon have to move back. I take my long hair out of its braid and comb my fingers through it as it dries.

"It's a kind of magical coal," explains Will, "from the caverns. We don't burn wood here in the Thorn because it would be disrespectful to the inhabitants." He motions to the trees around us.

As if on cue, a large form comes sliding out of the tree behind Will. "It took you long enough," hisses Dominus good-naturedly.

As usual, I am nervous around the huge creature, but the snake winks one jeweled eye at me and smiles his slow smile. He winds himself down to the ground and curls his body into a large red and gold pile. Even now, a good portion of him still ropes around the trunk of the tree above his head.

"We had a ways to come," Will motions to the cracked stone in the center of the pond. "Do you think it was noticeable?"

If Dominus had shoulders, he would shrug them. "I don't think ssso. I've kept a lookout and haven't ssseen anything unusssual all morning. We can ressst here for a while. Perhapsss Thea isss hungry."

My stomach growls. We hadn't had much breakfast.

"What time is it?"

The sun is high, and I am guessing it must be close to noon. I squint up at the trees above us and glimpse the blue of the sky. I had missed fresh air and real light. Will is rummaging through his pack, searching for the bread he had packed.

"It isss nearly one o'clock," says Dominus. "Where is the rest of our party?"

As if on cue, Ironsides appears on the surface of the pool and swims to the bank. Behind him, the water around the two pieces of the large stone bubbles. He crawls up the bank and over to where we sit. We all stare, as the cracked pieces of rock sink down beneath the pool. In a moment, they are gone, and the water moves over them with a slow roll as if they have never been.

Will gazes at Ironsides in admiration. The turtle manages to appear nonchalant. "A bit of help to cover our tracks should anyone come looking for us."

"Good idea, Ironsidess," says Dominus, but the turtle eyes the snake with suspicion.

"Oh, there you are. What have you to report?"

He speaks as a general to an under officer, and I cringe, hoping Dominus won't take offense. But the snake is amused.

"Nothing, jussst yet. The foressst hasss been quiet and pleasssant today. I was jussst sssaying Thea might be hungry," he motioned with his great head to Will and me, who are eating the bread despite it being sprinkled with sand.

"Where's Jack?" Iron nibbles a bit of the bread I drop for him but makes a face.

"Here," says Jack's voice, and he steps back into the clearing, out of breath.

"Hello, Dominus!"

He drops his hand on the snake's enormous head, like a man with his pet dog. The gesture is affection and the snake doesn't appear to mind. Jack turns to the rest of us.

"I did a wide sweep of the area and everything is all right for now, but we'd better get a move on. Are your clothes dry, your Highness?"

As usual, his tone sounds slightly exasperated when he speaks to me, as if I'm a child and a nuisance. He never calls me 'Thea', but only 'Your Highness', with the faintest trace of scorn in his voice. I swallow the lump of bread and sand and take a drink of water to rinse out my mouth.

"Thea." I say evenly, "And I think so."

I stand up and go over to my clothes. My cloak is still a bit damp, but the other things are nearly dry. I roll up my stockings and underthings and put them in my pack. I bring my boots nearer to the hot stones and braid my hair into a messy braid. I've lost the pins holding it up, so it will have to hang down.

The others are now looking at a map Jack has rolled out on the ground.

"We should go east," says Ironsides with authority. "It's the most direct route to the Old Road."

Dominus shakes his head. "The path may be watched," he argues. "We ssshould head sssouth and then east."

Will says nothing, but he is scared. He still doesn't like the idea of going on the Old Road.

"South takes us too close to the chasm," Jack says. "There may be a patrol."

Dominus and Ironsides glance at me.

"*I* don't know," I say. "Whatever everyone thinks is fine with me."

"Let's head a direct route," Jack says. "Straight east. Malius may know already which direction we are headed, so it won't matter much. We'll have to camp for the night somewhere, at any rate." He glances up at the sky through the trees.

Dominus again gives the impression of shrugging shoulders. His great neck ripples in interesting patterns. "I will go through the treetopsss."

He unwinds himself backward into the tree where his tail is still curled, his red and gold body graceful and powerful.

Will gathers up his fire-stones and puts them in his pack. When he touches them, they go dark and the heat recedes. He vanishes into the earth with a whoosh! only to appear on the other side of the clearing near a small opening in the trees.

Jack looks at me. I have finished putting my clothes away and am pulling on my boots.

"I'll go first. You and Iron follow me."

His words are an order and I start to retort but bite it back. I don't like it, but what can I do? I decide to try a different approach.

"How long until we make it to Lilywell?"

"At least two days," Jack is surprised by my quiet question. "It's deep in the Thorn."

I pick up Iron who perches himself on my shoulder. With a last glance at the clear pool, I follow Jack into the forest.

His broad back marches ahead of me. I tell myself I do not admire the muscles moving across his shoulders and the way his black hair falls across the nape of his neck. Vexed at myself, I look around instead.

I had thought the forest would be thick with trees and green-gold gloom, as it was when I had arrived, but here the bright sun shines down into large clearings. Long grass grows, tinted golden. Bluebells make a thick carpet for us to wade through. Giant trees stand alone, some with mossy undergrowth at their enormous roots.

Passing these, I turn my head. Small, glowing eyes watch us from under the gnarled roots. The eyes blink and fade away as I catch sight of them. The occasional twig falls as the great snake moves far overhead. I marvel at how quietly Dominus can travel and say so.

"He's skilled at not being seen or heard," agrees Jack. I wait for more, but Jack doesn't elaborate.

"What is the Old Road?"

We are moving deeper into the forest. Will strides alongside me, sometimes jumping into the earth and disappearing altogether. He pauses, mid-jump and comes down hard next to me.

"The Old Road is the Old Tournament Road. The King of Stoneham used to take it to the Tournament Fields every spring," he says, pushing his way through the tall grass. "It used to be a lovely road through the Thorn. Thornwoldians would line up along it to see the King pass by. The Road turned into a Faire in the heart of the forest with food stalls and people selling all kinds of things. It went all the way to tournament grounds. But after Malius took Stoneham it all stopped. It became overgrown. It's a shame. The Mudgluck carved some of the statues along it and did the gates as well."

"It sounds lovely," I agree. "I would have liked to have seen the tournaments."

Jack glances back over his shoulder at me, "You did. You don't remember them, I suppose."

He's right. I tried to imagine it. My parents and me, perhaps dozens of servants, riding in carriages along this road.

"There are no tournament fields now. I don't even think Malius remembers it exists. He was only at the tournaments once, and it was many years ago."

"I wouldn't be so certain Malius has forgotten the Old Road," Ironsides cautions. I glance around me, but there's nothing except trees and flowers and sunshine. It's hard to be afraid in such a beautiful place.

Hours pass. The sun dips down, slanting lower through the trees. None of us talk much. I am getting tired and thirsty. I take drinks from my water container and give Iron some too. Jack and Will have their own.

Will comes up out of the earth muddy and wet a few times, as if he has been playing in some underground stream. Jack's energy is endless. I long to stop and take a rest, but I hate the thought of his amused eyes on me, sizing me up as a weak girl. I grit my teeth and keep going. Iron rubs his head on my cheek.

When I am sure I can't take another step, Jack stops abruptly. I stumble backward in my effort not to run into him.

We have come to the end of the clearing and the tall grass. Before us is a wide opening into a sea of endless trees. This is the forest I remember from my first day. I peer ahead and follow Jack into the cool shadows.

Will takes the lead, dodging on ahead and muttering to himself. "Is this the right way? Second tree, right, two steps left. Down a hill and find the tree with the greenish colored bark." He hops on, following his own directions and leading us deep into the forest. Jack follows him, but at a slower pace, which I'm grateful for.

"Will knows the way better than any map, "whispers Iron. "His family is one of the Mudgluck families who built the Old Road."

The ground becomes a series of shallow plateaus heading downwards. It's a moment before I realize we are on a ruined staircase. It's overgrown with grass and moss and bracken, but the steps are still there. It feels as if it will never end, but at last it does.

Tangled branches shield the enormous stone arch. Beyond it, fallen logs lay across the faint trace of what had once been a smooth road of silvery stones. Grass grows between the cracks. Forest debris of twenty springs litter the ground. The path slides away into the forest, disappearing around a bend.

We hesitate, standing still in front of the ruins of delicate gates, now rusted and hanging sadly by broken hinges from each side of the arch. I walk over and examine the figures curled inside the gate's decorative work. People and animals are molded out of iron, their features obscured by corrosion. Over the arch, a metal sun twists its way up from the stone, its golden surface now tarnished and black. There are gaping holes where jewels were once set. Again, I look at the road beyond the arch. The trees throw long shadows across it.

"It looks darker in there," observes Will, voicing all of our thoughts.

Without a word, Dominus appears, winding his way down a nearby tree. He moves his enormous body over the ground through the ruined gates, peering up at the trees on either side of the road.

"Itsss much more overgrown than I remember. Thossse treessss come right the edge of the path now. They will help me ssstay clossse to you, your Highnessss."

He addresses me with a friendly flick of his long tongue, but I hang back, wrapping my cloak around myself and Ironsides. I have a strange fear of this crumbling, broken road I can't explain.

Dominus has moved himself slowly up the side of a great oak tree and half disappears into its leaves. Jack heaves his pack higher on his shoulder.

"Well, come on, your Highness," he says to me in his curt way, motioning me forward. He steps through the arch and hops over a small fallen tree in his way. He looks back at me, still standing palely by the ruined gate, and relents.

"It won't be long now until we can rest. We'll set up camp as soon as it gets dark." He motions at the sky.

The sun has sank well behind the trees. It won't be long until it is gone. I am determined not to appear cowardly in front of Jack. I take a deep breath and follow him, stepping around broken branches and loose stones. Will comes after me, even more reluctantly.

At first, it isn't so bad. The trees crowd close, but the light is soft, and the chirp of birds can be heard often. Slowly between the leaves, the shadows deepen. Every hour, gleaming eyes shine out at us, blinking wetly and vanishing, only to appear in another place.

I bite my lips and try not to stare. They are the same rounded eyes I had noticed earlier around the roots of the great trees, but larger. They frighten me with their strange, bulbous look. After an hour, they fade away and do not return.

The chirp of birds fades and an eerie silence creeps in. All we can hear are our own footsteps as we trod laboriously over the rough, uneven stones and climb over the trees laying in tangled heaps on the road.

There are stone statues among the trees near the side of the road, large pieces of shining rock carved with faces that leer, laugh, or cry, according the artist's whim. Each statue holds an iron lantern, set firmly into the rock, the glass broken and the flame lifeless.

Will is cheered up at the sight of these. "Will you look at them?" He pokes at my boot. "And those? What workmanship! Beautiful!"

Years ago, with the road clear of debris, the trees pushed back, and golden light spilling forth from shining glass and iron, the statues must have been interesting and amusing objects, but here, in the fading light and looming dark they are frightening things.

The oppressiveness grows. There are sounds. A soft rustling from the trees on either side of us. Above, Dominus glides smoothly, barely stirring a leaf. I can't see him. Maybe he has gone on ahead. The rustling sounds grow louder and still there is no end to the endless, worn path of silvery dust and the thick trees.

"How long is this Old Road?"

The sound of my own voice breaking the heavy, muted silence and soft rustling in the undergrowth makes me more frightened.

Jack turns and looks around at the growing dusk. "Half a day's journey until we can get off it and make our way to –"

He stops and says nothing more, his eyes widening as he clamps his mouth shut. He nearly said our destination aloud and he is afraid of being overheard. A shudder goes through me.

We go on.

There are snaps of branches off to my right. Each time one comes, a loud crack in the thick stillness, I jump and cause Ironsides to grip my shoulder tight with his sharp claws.

"Ow," I complain, picking him up and moving him to my other shoulder. "Give that side a rest, won't you?"

"Stop jumping," mutters Ironsides, but he is looking around and his eyes are enormous. This reminds me of the strange, yellow eyes. I ask him about them in a low tone.

"Shhh – "He admonishes me in a whisper and shakes his head. "There are some things best left to a warm fire inside thick walls. When we reach Broon's, I will tell you about them."

If we reach Broon's, I think. Will stops. I nearly trip over him as I pull myself up short.

"What is it?" asks Ironsides in a low tone. I am alarmed to find it's dark now. A faint pink light is shining between the leaves as the sun sinks, but here in the forest night has come.

Iron's voice cuts through the silence. "Jack, we need to rest. We can't go on much longer."

I glance at Iron, noting he has not said my name. Jack pauses and I think he isn't going to respond, but he turns and comes back toward us.

"We need to get off this road," whispers Iron to Jack.

"It might not be anything," murmurs Jack in response, but he looks up.

"Dominus!"

Dominus's head appears above us from out of the leaves.

"Yesss?"

"We need to make camp for the night. Do you see a good spot anywhere?"

Dominus head disappears. Around us the silence deepens. In a few moments Dominus is back, dropping out of the trees smoothly.

Motioning for us to follow, he heads off the road to our left in a zig zag pattern. We leave the path and enter the forest. It is extremely dark here, but I am immediately struck by the sensation of no longer being watched. The relief is so great I want to laugh. Jack makes a gesture and a small light glows from his hand. It flickers and casts a circle of light around us so we can see a few steps ahead of us.

"Quickly," he whispers, and we move.

After a time, we come to a circle of giant trees growing closely together. We slip between them and find ourselves in a large clearing. The clearing has a few fallen trees in it, creating a triangle of extra protection. Above us, the moon shines down softly. Around us, the trees make a nearly solid wall. Jack extinguishes the light.

"Here. We'll be safe enough here until morning."

Will busies himself laying out his fire stones. They glow yellow, giving off the marvelous heat.

I drop to the ground next to them, so exhausted I can't move. I want to wrap my cloak around me and go to sleep, but Iron's head nudges my cheek.

"You must eat something, Thea."

"All right. But not sandy bread again."

Jack overhears me and chuckles. Will is abashed.

"I can't help it," he mutters. "It's what Mudgluck's eat."

"But not humans," I say, giggling. "I was picking sand out of my teeth for miles."

Jack has taken a pan from his pack and a small portable grate. He lays these over the fire and takes out a few eggs and a slab of bacon. Dominus disappears through a gap in the trees.

"He's off to hunt his own dinner," says Jack, and Iron shudders.

I go through my pack and find some dried fruit. This I give to Iron, who eats it gratefully. Will is munching his Mudgluck bread and this time he has smeared it with something that appears to be mud and wet weeds.

I turn to my own plate of eggs and bacon and waste no time in devouring the meal. It's delicious. When we are finished, Jack makes some more, and we eat that too. Finally, I sit back against one of the convenient fallen logs with a sigh.

Jack is sitting across from me, wrapped in his cloak. His eyes blink in the faint glow of the non-fire. Dominus has returned, sliding back into the clearing, and coiling himself near us with his head on Jack's knee. As before, I am reminded of a giant lapdog. He closes his emerald eyes.

Iron has gotten down from my shoulder and has curled up closer to the log, withdrawing his head and feet. A small snore issues from his shell. Will is asleep on his back, muddy crumbs on his shirt.

I wrap my cloak closer around me.

"It's all right, your Highness," says Jack, "Go ahead and sleep. You must be tired."

"Thea."

But he's right. I curl up next to Iron's shell and fall asleep and dream.

I am wandering in a dark stone passageway. I think it's somewhere in Ember's cavern, but the walls around me are wet with a dark liquid. When I touch it, it buzzes on my hand. I draw back from it and keep going. Far away, a voice calls my name. Thea! it says, and I freeze. The voice is my Papa's voice. I run, my shoes catching on the uneven floor. Heavy skirts and soft shoes hinder me. I'm dressed in a dress a princess might wear in a fairy tale. One Cinderella might wear to her ball. Unused to it, I struggle to move quickly. Again my name is called. Thea! This time, my Papa's voice is strained and raw as if something is holding his throat, choking him. Someone screams.

With a gasp I sit up and open my eyes. Jack's steady gray eyes are watching me across the glowing stones.

"Are you all right, your Highness?" he asks softly.

"A bad dream." I can still feel the weight of the dress and the buzz of the strange liquid on my hands.

"Go back to sleep," Jack says. "Everything is fine."

"I don't want to."

I am embarrassed. Would he think I'm a child? Afraid of bad dreams? "Tell me things," I hear myself say. "Things about yourself."

"What do you want to know?" He is surprised and suspicious.

"I don't know."

He laughs at me. "It's not a good start, your Highness."

"Seriously," I say, irritated. "Why don't you call me Thea? I'm not a Highness anything."

I glare at the glowing magical coals.

Jack is quiet for a minute. "But you are Her Royal Highness. Even if you don't feel it yet." His voice is odd. It is both bitter and amused. I bristle.

"I don't want to. I want —"

I stop. I don't know what I want anymore. I have wanted several things since getting old enough to want things, but none of them have worked out. I think about learning to be Abigail's apprentice and failing at it, and about Ember teaching me how to use my ability to see magic. I scowl at the ground.

"Okay. Thea."

The way he says my name makes me flush, but not with anger.

"I suppose you've heard about my unfortunate past?" His voice is quiet.

"I haven't."

"Oh."

I can tell he doesn't want to tell me about it, but I'm curious. "Why is it unfortunate?"

"I'm a jinx," says Jack, and for the first time he sounds like a young man, not a soldier giving orders.

"Why should you be?"

Jack snorts. "You don't know the story?"

I shake my head.

Jack makes a resigned motion with his head. He gets up and comes over to sit next to me, sinking gracefully to the ground. He wraps his cloak around himself tighter.

"Fine. I'll tell you, but then you must get some sleep."

I curl up in my own cloak, my eyes fixed on him.

"Where to start?" he muses. "I guess I'll begin by saying Broon raised me and he taught me everything I know, except how to fight. I had to run away to learn."

The noise he gives is a bit rueful. "Broon always says the problems of a world cannot be solved with violence. I don't know whether I agree with him or not," he adds. "I didn't agree with him at the time, but now I'm not so sure. Because Serafin died."

This rings a faint bell. "Serafin? One of the council members Ironsides mentioned?"

"Serafin was Captain of a ship. *The Homecoming.* I ran away and joined his crew when I was fourteen. He taught me everything he knew about sailing, and fighting, and how to lead men. When he was killed last spring —"

Jack stops and pulls his sword from its scabbard. He holds it out to me, and I take it. A spark runs up my arm as I turn the cold and heavy blade from side to side. The sharp edge of it catches the faint moonlight and gleams like fine silver thread.

"It's his own sword," Jack gazes at it with a mixed expression. "He gave it to me as he lay dying."

His voice is gruff, as if he is trying to talk around something hurting him. He takes the sword from me and puts it back into its worn scabbard.

I pretend not to see him wipe his eyes on his sleeve. Most of the village boys in Brell would have died before letting a girl see them cry.

"I'm sorry, Jack," I say to the non-fire. "My parents died when I was ten."

He nods, wiping his hand across his eyes briefly, "Serafin and Broon were the only parents I've ever known. I never knew my mother or my father."

"Why?"

"I don't know exactly. Well. I don't know part of it. Dominus told me what he knows about the story when I was a kid, even though maybe he shouldn't have."

"Dominus!"

"Yes, Dominus."

He regards me with an odd expression. "It's not a happy story. Are you sure you want to know?"

"Yes," I say promptly, and he goes on with reluctance.

"My mother was a plainswoman from a tribal people. They live on the Glasshedge Moors between the Light and Dark Mountains and the Glass Sea. Of course, they don't call it Glasshedge, that's a Thornwoldian name. Their name for it is Datura, which is a kind of flower growing there. They are proud and live well in a harsh environment. The snake has a special meaning to them. It represents life and death and rebirth. Snakes shed their skin you know. Snakes are shown tattooed on the arms of their gods."

He glances at Dominus's sleeping form and I think I understand the friendship between them.

"Dominus was a sort of god to them?"

Jack laughs softly. "No, no. Dominus was born not long before I was. He is one of the great snakes of the Datura, the ones held sacred by my mother's people. There are few of his kind left. He's special, but not a god of any kind."

I settle back as Jack goes on.

"As I said, my mother was a woman of the tribes of Datura. She was a Chief's daughter, and by all accounts she was beautiful and courageous, with a gentle heart. When she was eighteen, a young man came across the Glasshedge Moors to her village. He had been wandering lost for some time and was very weak. With him was a large snake." Jack motions to Dominus.

"Dominus had the good – or bad – luck of being acquired by this man and trained as a kind of companion. Naturally, my mother's people saw the snake, noticed how it stayed near him, and thought the young man must be special. They took him in, and my mother's family nursed him back to health. When he was better, he told them he was a scholar, headed for the Light and Dark Mountains to study with the people there."

I sit up with an intake of breath.

"Yes," he says. "It was Malius they had found and saved."

"And Dominus was his friend?"

"Servant," Jack says. He points to Dominus's sleeping form. "See the scars on his back?"

Dominus has white scarring along his neck and back.. I remember what Ember said. Ember said the scars didn't get there by accident.

"My mother noticed the scars too. She was kind to Dominus and often protected him from Malius. Which would serve her well later on, because as it turns out, Malius and my mother fell in love."

I stare at him. Jack is the son of Malius.

In a flash, I remember the night on the road in Brell. The stranger's face. Malius's face. Jack has the same strong chin. The same full lips. I glance down at his hands. Jacks hands are beautifully shaped, but weathered and rough.

Jack is bitter. "Yes. I'm the only living bastard of Malius, ruler of Stoneham, and am therefore supposed to be a traitor or worse."

I have no idea what to say.

"As if I could," Jack is looking away from me. "I have heard my whole life how I'm the son of the evil Malius and most people hate me because of it."

I find my voice. "I know."

Jack glares at me. "You can't know."

"I do," I insist. "No one liked me in Brell because I was different. They were terrible to me in school. They called me witch-girl and used to hit me with stones. I've never had a single friend my own age."

He looks at me, measuring my words. He's quiet so long I am not sure he believes me, but he finally shakes his head.

"We are two of a kind, I guess."

I curl up again, leaning on my fallen log. "But you had Dominus. How did that happen if he was Malius's servant?"

Jack is quiet for a minute. "This is the sad part. Are you sure you want to hear?"

What he has to tell me can't be worse than anything I've heard since I arrived in Thornwold. I nod.

"Malius stayed with the tribe. He learned their ways and seemed to respect them. Perhaps he even thought he loved my mother. But Malius had flashes of rage. He used to beat Dominus. My mother would get in the way and try and stop him, often taking the beating herself."

Jack clenches his fists. "In time, she was pregnant with me. But as we know, Malius was on a quest for revenge and only wanted more power. He wasn't content to stay in the Datura, and it didn't suit him to be saddled with a wife and child. So one night he left. That's all. My mother woke and he was gone. She went home to her family. I was born a few months later. When I was about a year old, my mother set off for the Light and Dark Mountains, where she knew my father had gone."

"But how could she follow him?" I ask. "If he beat her? And what about you?"

"I wish I knew. She took me with her," he adds. "Because she never came back to Datura. Neither did I, until many years later."

My mouth is dry. "What happened?"

"When my mother found him, Malius was furious, but he pretended to be fine with it. He was in the middle of his studies and getting closer to finding the Globe's location. He didn't want anything stopping him." Jack begins to speak faster as if to get this part of the story over with.

"One day, Malius told Dominus to stay behind while he and my mother and I went for a walk into the hills. Dominus had a terrible feeling. As I've said, he was fond of my mother. So he went after them, but he was too late. Malius had strangled my mother and was turning on me. Dominus silently came up behind him and smashed the back of his master's head with his enormous tail. It didn't kill Malius. It only knocked him out. Pity."

"Jack," I am horror-struck. "Oh Jack –"

"I was only one. I don't remember a thing. As for my mother, it was too late. She was dead and I was crying. Dominus picked me up and left the Mountains for good. He didn't know where to go, but he made his way to a village near Stoneham. The villagers were shocked to see a giant snake with a baby, but they took us in and cared for us. One day, Broon came striding into the village and asked to see me. He invited us both to live with him in Lilywell. That's all."

His story ends abruptly. I can't stop seeing the image of her, his beautiful mother, eyes open, but staring at nothing and reflecting only the sky, while her baby boy cried next to her lifeless body and Malius looked coldly down at them both.

"How terrible," I say. "Your poor mother."

Jack puts his hand on my shoulder, pulling me out of my head full of ghastly images. "It's okay, Thea. It was a long time ago."

His face is close to mine, but he doesn't move away. His eyelashes are long, and his eyes are gray and soft. We stare at each other. His hand on my shoulder is like a heavy, warm weight.

A scream rips out of the darkness.

I jump. The dark coals are still glowing. Ironsides shell moves, and his blinking eyes emerge. I want to imagine the scream is not real, an echo of my nightmare, but it comes again.

Jack has leaped to his feet. Dominus has lifted his great head and is looking as serious as it is possible for a snake with a curving mouth to look.

"We were being followed," he hisses in a low tone. "For sssome milesss. When we got off the road, I thought we were sssafe enough."

"Stay here," Jack orders us, and is gone.

I glare after him before scrambling to my feet too. "I'm going with him."

Before Dominus or a sleepy Will or a dazed Ironsides can protest, I am through the narrow gap in the protective circle of trees and out in the forest, running after Jack. I catch up with him when he pauses near a clump of bushes.

"I told you to stay there!" he whispers, furious.

"I'm capable of fighting too," I hiss back at him. "If it comes to a fight."

Before he can answer me the scream comes again. It sounds as if its overhead. I move to look up, but Jack pulls me down and grabs my hood, yanking it up to cover my face.

"It's a scout," he says in my ear. "Keep your head down. Faces show up in the dark."

Trying not to think about his warm breath on my ear, or the strength of his arm around my shoulders, I keep my head down. We breathe, listening. After a few minutes, the scream comes a third time. This time its farther away. Jack releases me slowly. As we part, I am shaky.

"Keep your hood up, "he orders. "And your head down."

"Fine," I snap in a whisper. "But I'm coming with you."

"Good" he says, surprising me. "Because we are going back to camp."

Am I imagining it or is there a faint note of admiration in his voice? I smile to myself and follow him back to the clearing.

"Dominus," says Jack, as we enter the circle of trees. "You have to tell me when we are being followed. In the future, you'll let me know as soon as possible." He glares at the snake.

The snake is abashed, but his emerald eyes gleam. He slides over to me as I pick up Ironsides and put him on my shoulder.

"Are you all right, your Highnessss?"

"I'm okay. But shouldn't we get out of here?"

I strap my pack together, making sure I have everything. Will has put the coals and the cooking items away, and is looking worriedly from tree to tree, muttering to himself.

Jack is still glowering. "Dominus! Report!"

"There were Watchersss," His giant head is still near mine. His tongue flicks playfully out of his mouth and grazes my nose.

My heart is pounding with rising panic, but as his tongue tickles me, I choke back a hysterical laugh.

"The sun wasss ssstill up. I took count. There were a few at firssst, tracking usss. We knew the Watchersss are everywhere. We knew it wasss a risssk. I'm sssory. I should have sssaid sssomething, but I hoped perhapsss they were on our sssside."

Will snorts at this, but the snake ignores him. "I hoped at leasst they were neutral and were merely following usss out of curiosssity, but I fear it isss not ssso. They all fell back when we left the Road."

He pauses and flicks his tongue again, his eyes gleaming even more brightly. "Perhaps becaussse one or two of their number went missssing."

Jack is pacing. He isn't angry now. "Now the scout. It means Malius's men will be on our trail soon enough."

"So, it begins," says Iron. He is fierce. "Jack, we must make it to Broon's borders as fast as we can."

"The Watcher's will tell them," whispers Will. He has turned away from the trees and is shaking. Dust is coming off his small form. "They will know we left the Old Road here."

"It can't be helped," says Dominus. "Now let uss go ssswiftly."

He turns and nudges me. "Jack and Will firssst," he says. "Then you and Ironsssidess. I will come behind you."

I am quivering from head to foot, but I say nothing and follow Jack and Will out of the clearing and through the enormous trees. My heart is pounding as my eyes adjust to the gloom. I stumble along in Jack and Will's wake, praying we can make the miles we need to make before Malius sends his soldiers after us. The moon has set, but dawn is coming.

We have barely left the clearing behind when a piercing whistle rips through the night, shattering the darkness with a warning sound. I whirl and look back. Through the gap in trees I can make out several figures moving in unison. Malius's soldiers.

FIRE AND SILVER

Are they men? They are larger than ordinary men, encased in armor and silent. Their masked faces turn to look at us as Jack flashes past me, drawing his sword. They move as one, in lines of three, one at their head. They draw their swords and march toward us, crushing the earth beneath iron feet.

"Run!" screams Jack at me. "For god sake, Thea!"

The sound of his voice sends the blood and energy churning through me, and I turn and run.

Glancing back, I see Dominus has reared his enormous head and is poised for attack. Jack is holding Serafin's sword. They are so small. The ugly silver-white color of fear swirls around them both.

I skid to a stop.

Iron gasps in my ear, "Oh no, Thea!"

I ignore him. I turn back and assess the situation. Moving to the left, I get clear of Jack and Dominus, so I am facing the oncoming soldiers from the side. They are nearly on top of my companions now. I hold my hands together in the way Ember showed me back in the cavern.

"Hang on, Iron" I say, ignoring his moan of anxiety.

I close my eyes and focus my breathing. The first ball of light hits the man in front with a flash of brilliant blue. He stops, his armor glowing as cracks appear all over it. He shatters, crumbling to pieces with a roar.

There is a yell from Jack, and I turn as he strikes another solider, who hasn't hesitated at all at the death of the leader. The soldier crumbles as Jack's sword touches him.

108

Dominus swings his head and knocks another of them to the side. The flash of the soldier's sword slices through the air as the soldier goes flying into a tree. The tree swings one of its branches downward, breaking the head off the soldier's body of armor. It rolls to the side, empty. Dominus has dropped to the ground and lays still.

I barely have time to register this as I take aim and focus another stream of blue magic. This one swings wide to avoid Jack's head by an inch and hits another of the steadily marching soldiers. He explodes with the same cracked light.

Will has vanished to earth, but now appears directly under the feet of the last line of three soldiers. He throws the earth up and they topple. Even as I move forward, the surrounding trees move in, their giant roots pushing through the earth and wrapping around the iron legs and arms of the soldiers, pulling them apart, dragging them under the earth. With a ground-shaking roar, the trees push them down, and the surge of loose dirt knocks me to my knees.

Everything is dark and silent. There is a whoop of laughter, and Will comes bouncing toward me.

"All right, Thea!" he says. "That was amazing shooting!"

"What do you mean?" I gasp. "It was fast thinking on your part! And the trees?"

Before he can answer, Jack strides forward, looking stern. "I told you to run," he snaps, pulling me roughly to my feet.

"There were too many of them," I point out. "I told you I don't have trouble throwing magic!"

We glare at each other, but Ironsides, breathing heavily, says, "She helped, Jack. Now, look at Dominus."

The great snake is lying where he fell, his beautiful eyes shut. His neck is bleeding heavily. The sword I saw flying through the air must have struck him.

In a flash Jack is next to him, white-faced, holding his head. "My brother," he says, his voice shaking.

I grab my pack and rush over, fumbling for Ember's silver flask of healing liquid. Finding it, I pour a few drops of it on the wound. It heals. I wipe some of the blood away and Dominus opens his emerald eyes.

"Thank you," he murmurs. He flicks his long tongue at Jack as if to assure the young man he is fine.

"Anyone else?" I ask, holding up the vial, but everyone shakes their head.

The tree's branch which had struck and decapitated the soldier is hanging by a few twists of bark. I walk over to it and sprinkle a few drops of the liquid on the branch. For a moment, nothing happens. Then the tree shudders and the bark winds itself back together. In a few moments, the branch is whole and lifts gently into the air. The tree drops a small shower of leaves on me, as if in thanks. I pat its trunk gently.

"You didn't have to do that," says Jack. He's still holding Dominus's head in his arms. "Trees heal themselves."

"It didn't have to help us, either" I point out. "But it did."

I turn and look at the group of trees. "Thank you all."

The trees don't speak of course, but they are listening.

"A true ruler of the Thorn," Ironsides says so quietly I nearly miss it. He is smiling to himself. I roll my eyes and pick up my pack.

"We ssshould get moving," says Dominus. "I don't like it. It wasss only ssseven of them. It'sss wrong."

The sun is rising now, its first early rays are touching the tops of the trees and the air turns silver as it catches the dew.

"Are you okay to move?" Jack says to Dominus, looking worried.

"Yesss, I'm fine," he smiles his curved mouth at me. "Thanks to you, Highnessss."

I smile back at him and open my mouth to speak, but there is a low rumble, like distant thunder. It comes from behind us.

I am puzzled, but Jack has whirled around and is staring back at the dense forest behind us. There isn't anything but silent trees and silvery air.

The sound comes again. It's getting closer. Everyone is looking behind us. I squint up into the treetops, noting their color is different; a darker green. Abruptly, the ground shakes, waves of vibrations coming out of the forest and moving past us.

Dominus is winding himself up the trunk of a tree. His head disappears into its leaves. On the ground, we wait.

High in the air, Dominus lifts his enormous head to the early morning sky and breaths in. The wind blows a strange scent and far away to the south, the great snake observes the edge of the forest and a faint gleam of high black towers.

Wait. Not towers. Towers don't move. The soot black head rises from the trees, smoke seeping from its nostrils, red eyes gleaming. The snake pulls his head back down into the leaves, but the dragon is already moving in their direction. His enormous roar fills the air. With each step, the ground shakes. He's moving slowly, crushing trees with each step, bark and branches flying into the air behind him. His head and eyes are focused downward, so he hasn't spotted Dominus.

The great snake gazes to the west, where the forest runs down into a valley. There, a few miles away from them, was the heart of the Thorn and safety. With a last look at the enormous black beast, he drops out of the tree and to the ground.

"An ash dragon," says Dominus as soon as he's on the ground.

Jack's eyes widen. He wheels on me instantly, where I am standing white-faced gaping at the snake.

"We have to go now," he orders. "Thea, whatever happens, stay calm. When I tell you to run this time, you must run. No arguments."

I shake my head numbly. "I—" I begin, but the ground shakes again. The sound vibrates the air.

"Hear that? Those are only his steps. He can wipe us out with one breath. Your magic won't work on this dragon. Dominus, how far away are we?"

I think it's odd Jack wants to know how far away we are. Why not ask how far away the dragon is? But Dominus understands.

"A mile eassst."

He winds his way up the trunk of the tree again, pausing before his head disappears. "Lesss than a half an hour if you move quickly. I'm going ahead. I can move fassster and get help."

"Help from where?" I ask, but Will jumps to his feet.

"Me too," the Mudgluck says. "Which way?"

"Straight east," says Jack. "We're right behind you."

Will leaps into the earth and is gone.

"Help from where?" I ask again. Jack ignores me.

"The borders of Lilywell are only a few miles more," explains Iron. "If we get there, we are safe."

I don't see how borders can protect us from a fire breathing dragon, but I don't say this.

"Can't we hide?" I say instead. I point around to the trees, "Surely it can't see us if we hide somewhere?"

"Dragons have a keen sense of smell," says Iron, before Jack can speak. "All that fire, clears the sinuses."

Normally, I would laugh at this, but I am terrified. Jack has gathered up his pack and strapped it securely to himself. His eyes are blazing. He grabs my hand.

"Now, Thea," he says. "Run."

We run.

I keep hoping I will wake up, sure this can't be happening, certain it is all a nightmare. I have no words to tell you what it is to run through an enchanted forest knowing a fire-breathing monster is behind you, sniffing for your scent, shaking the ground with each step. It is the most terrifying thing you can imagine.

Every few minutes, the ground quakes as the dragon takes a step closer to us. Branches and leaves shower down on us.

Jack and I stumble and nearly fall. Once, when this happens, I do fall and Ironsides loses his hold on my shoulder. He goes flying into some undergrowth. I scream for Jack and go after the turtle, sobbing and searching through the bracken.

Luckily, in moments, I find him. I pick him up, ignoring his protests, and shove him into my pack. Inside he will be safe.

Jack grabs my hand and again we are off. I make up my mind to throw the pack with Ironsides in it as far away from me as I can when the dragon comes bursting out of the trees above us.

We run and run. The smell of smoke and ash hangs in the air around us. The earth-shaking steps crash louder and louder. Jack yells my name. Far ahead, there is a break in the trees.

"See it," he yells in my ear. "Get there! That's the boundary. We're nearly there!"

Ten steps, twenty, thirty. A pain rips my side. Another shake splits the air so fiercely the trees around us bend to earth, and I am flung to one side as Jack is flung to the other. I land on my back, wedged up against a mossy log.

Staring up, dizzy, I think the sky has gone black. But the world comes into focus and I am staring at the underside of the dragon. Its great belly and neck tower over me. It lowers its head and looks at me. My white face is reflected in its red eye. The smell of smoke is choking me.

I close my eyes, waiting for fire, for pain, for death, but I sense its head recede. A strange trumpeting sound comes from the creature instead. A shower of sparks falls around me, and I open my eyes.

Jack is standing in front of me, his sword raised. The dragon has raised its long neck and is roaring into the sky. Sparks and fire shoot high above him. Ash, sparks, and debris rain around us both.

"Run, Thea," screams Jack, his voice sounding far away. "Run!"

But I cower where I sit. My legs are water and I can't move.

The dragon lowers its head, swooping through the trees, breaking branches, and dropping burning embers. It stares at Jack and me, smoke seeping from its enormous teeth. It grins.

The world slows. I am aware of every blade of grass beneath my fingers, every ache in my body, every bit of sweat running down my face. The air around us pauses.

Jack's mouth is open. He is screaming, but all I can hear is the deep ashen breath of the giant and the intense silence of the forest around us. I cannot look away from its red eye rimmed with gold.

The dragon is gone.

A light, brilliant and blinding, sweeps between us and the monster. It ripples in the sunlight. It hits the dragon with such force the huge animal falls back, disappearing from view. Jack throws me down, his body covering mine, pushing my face into the moss beneath us. Branches, embers, and ash rain down on us.

I can't breathe, but Jack is on his feet, yanking me up, dragging me at a run toward the line of trees, which is still there. Everything is still here. We're still here. There is a roaring so loud it hurts my ears, but it is farther away now and far overhead.

Jack and I burst through the trees and there is a pop, breaking into frigid mountain air from a sweltering jungle. The air snaps into clearness. We're in a large open meadow surrounded by forest.

113

Dominus is in the middle of the field, waving his enormous head wildly in our direction.

"Get to the other ssside," he roars, and we sprint by him, heading toward the line of trees across from us. He follows us.

Hooded figures emerge from the woods and step out onto the field. They have bows and arrows pointed at the sky. I slow, but Jack grabs my hand and pulls me toward them.

"It's all right, Thea," he yells. "Keep going!"

My ears are ringing. We run through the figures and into the trees. Behind us, there is a burst of heat so intense that I am thrown from my feet again.

This time, I barely touch the ground before I am up again. I turn back toward the meadow and a wall of flame is burning. I barely take this in before it is extinguished in a shower of silver.

Broon is beside me, huge and powerful, striding toward the open meadow. His eyes are alight with rage. I am pushed aside, and Jack catches me by the elbow before I fall. He drags me back into the trees farther away from the field, but we're still able to see what's happening. My eyes are fixed on Broon as he walks out onto the field.

As he looks up, so do I. Above us, the great black dragon is hovering alongside a smaller silver dragon. The two creatures are circling each other, bursts of flame from one, burst of white-hot silver from the other.

My eyes widen. Ember is astride Lucius. The Lady of Fire is shooting flame from her hands, as the living silver dragon is fiercely fighting the huge black dragon.

From my pack, still securely attached to my shoulder, Iron's head emerges. He stares up at the two dragons and the small form of Ember. Will comes out of the earth and stands at my feet, looking terrified. Dominus has stopped near the edge of the meadow. He is half-reared up on his powerful body, sitting among the hooded archers who have retreated into the edges of the trees. Everyone is watching Broon or Ember and the dragons.

The black dragon roars a wall of smoking flame at Lucius. Lucius dodges and counters with a silver jet of light. Ember throws a wall of pure red flame. The light and fire meets and whirls around all three. The black dragon screams in frustration, causing everyone on the ground to cower. Everyone except

Broon.

The giant man stands, his hood thrown back, his dark green cloak shimmering around him. He raises a hand. From it shoots a silver net of light. It spreads itself, rocketing toward the black dragon.

The monster dodges it neatly. Shuffling out of the way in the air, it bares its teeth and blows a gigantic breath of flame toward Broon, who raises his arm and blocks it casually, as if it were a fly. The fire bounces back toward the black dragon, who sidesteps again.

Broon straightens up. His face changes expression. He opens his mouth, but I can't hear what he is saying because Ember and Lucius have come out of nowhere and are charging.

An arrow of silver, Lucius comes zooming toward his enemy, a stream of white fire from his mouth. Ember stands up on his back, her arms outstretched, her figure steady as she balances herself. She is cloaked in red and her dark hair is coming loose around her.

The black dragon turns a half a second too late. White flame and red flame catches one wing. With a scream of fury and pain, the black dragon is thrown on his back in the air, and falters. Ember and Lucius soar over him with a flip of the silver dragon's magnificent tail. The hooded men on the ground cheer.

But the black dragon is not finished. It rights itself quickly, despite the burning wing, and chases the silver dragon and the Lady of Fire. With an enormous breath, it blows a stream of fire so massive it lights the sky, blending with the shimmering morning air and gray smoke.

On the ground, I know what's going to happen a moment before it does. My voice is screaming for Ember, right before the massive fire from the black smoking dragon momentarily blinds everyone and we cover our eyes.

As the flame engulfs Lucius and Ember, the silver dragon freezes in the air, silver white and shining. His head turns helplessly toward Ember, as if looking for instruction. Ember, sitting on his back, throws her arms forward as if to cradle his head. Protective light shoots out of her, but it is too late.

The living silver dragon liquifies. His outline lingers, his beautiful head and wings and shining tail frozen against a

115

background of smoke, and then silver liquid pours down from the sky into the meadow, where it pools and smokes on the blackened ground, sinking into the earth.

Ember, still glowing with protective light, is falling through the sky. As Lucius dissolves, Broon throws an arm upward, catching her and slowing her fall. He brings her gently to earth. She lays still, her slumped form small and insignificant in the spot where the remains of Lucius have disappeared.

Iron gives a cry and Will swears. A shout of rage goes up among the hooded men, but Broon's face is unreadable and set. He gazes up at the black dragon, who is now whirling above him, its mouth stretched, teeth bared in a grin.

Broon lifts his hands into the sky. A humming sound vibrates the air. In the trees around us, the leaves are shining with a golden light. The trunks of trees are glowing. Quickwillow are emerging from the roots and branches, their colors shining so bright I can't look at them. Broon brings his hands down in a swift motion and a golden circle of light shoots out from his body.

Everyone ducks as the light comes shooting toward us. I cover my face as it passes through Jack and me. Its energy is so strong it knocks us to the ground.

It echoes away from us, and leaves everything deadly still. Black soot and ash is pouring from the sky where the monster had been. It hits the ground with a thud, sliding over the field and blackening the grass. Some of it slides over the still body of Ember.

No one cheers. There is silence. We are all staring at the giant figure of Broon, now covered in ashes, in the middle of the field. He gazes down at his giant hands and brings them up to cover his face.

Jack is pulling me to my feet and hugging me to him as I sob in relief. He is murmuring something, but I can't hear what it is because inexplicably the air shimmers in front of us and a musty scent picks its way through the smoke.

The hooded figure of a man is standing in front of us, his handsome features distorted by rage. The color swirling out of him is the strange color I've seen twice before. He glares at me but then he looks at Jack. The color around him vanishes, as if in surprise.

116

White-faced, Jack stares at his father. They do resemble each other, but Jack's gray eyes are soft and human. Malius is handsome, but there's something in his face, a tautness stretches over his features. His eyes are mine, but they are cold.

Behind him, there is a shout and Broon is striding from the field toward us, his giant form furious and threatening. Dragon's ashes stream off him in a haze. Malius gazes from Jack to me and his face is a mask. With a flip of his cloak, he disappears into the air.

LILYWELL

Passing under the arch of tangled wood, we follow a smooth path of golden dust and find the setting sun lingering on cascading pools of water covered in lilies.

Broon's house sits in a clearing, surrounded by high gates of wood and stone. The stone lies in varying patterns, and the wood splitting it grows in smooth curves. Each thick post of wood intertwines with another, creating gates unlike any I have ever seen.

The house is made of trees growing together, molding one to another until they make a solid wall, bent by the curve of a knot or a tree trunk. Here and there, a light gleams out at us from narrow gaps.

The roof of the house is woven from branches and leaves. These are laced tight, creating a shield against the elements. A bridge of worn stone leads the way over water and up wooden steps to a green door. On the door hangs a large brass knocker with a face resembling the ones cut into stone on the Old Road. It grins at us. Above the door hangs a lantern of green glass, glowing with a beautiful light.

After the disaster at the meadow, and after Malius disappeared, the men in brown hoods had rushed toward Ember's still form. One of them gave a shout telling us she was all right, just knocked out. I was relieved she wasn't dead.

Broon had strode over to us and grasped Jack by his shoulders.

"My son," he said and hugged him. Watching them, I wanted to cry.

Jack's face was white, but he smiled at Broon. "It's good to see you," was all he said.

Will was sitting at my feet, crying. I leaned over and hugged him. "Poor Lucius," he said. "Poor, poor Lucius."

Iron, who had no real love for the living silver dragon and was very worried about Ember, was furious. "This is an outrage," he blustered. "What was that giant black thing?"

Broon sighed. "A manifestation Dragon," he explained. "Malius started using them as soon as he took over. He conjures them out of smoke and ash and infuses them with power. They do his bidding. They scout for him, hunt for him, lay waste to villages for him to teach his subjects a lesson. They kill for him when necessary."

At the word 'scout' I glanced at Jack, horrified. Was that what had been tracking us and screamed overhead early this morning?

"We heard it this morning," he said, confirming my thought. "It was flying over us."

The men had created a makeshift stretcher for Ember, and now brought it to where we were, laying her carefully down. She was pale, her beautiful, sparkling-glass skin tarnished and dim, but otherwise unharmed. Iron crept over to her and sat on her arm.

"She'll be all right," he said, more to himself than to me. "She's the Lady of Fire, so fire can't hurt her."

Broon knelt next to her. "Dragon fire is a bit different, Iron," he said.

He crooned a strange song at her. I could see a stream of orange and gold swirl out of his mouth and around us. It dropped toward her and caressed her face. The small frown on her brow smoothed out. The colors rose and wound their way among the Quickwillow, who hovered anxiously nearby, before fading in the air. Broon stroked her dark hair.

"She'll sleep peacefully now," he said, and I looked at him.

"She only needs rest," he assured me. "Luckily, she wasn't burned. Four of the Thornmen can manage her easily."

He gestured and four of the men in brown hoods came over and lifted her stretcher carefully onto their shoulders. Iron stayed

119

on Ember's arm.

"You going to be okay up there?" I called. There was no response, but what I could see of his back clawed foot gave a small stamp.

Dominus approached Broon, winding his enormous head up through the air until he was as tall as the giant man.

"Broon," he hissed, with a glance at a group of Broon's archers standing near us. The men don't appear to be listening. "There were Watchersss following usss on the Old Road."

"It isn't unusual. The Watchers are in their domain. They are here in my lands. They have a right to observe anyone they choose. It is written."

"A right to obssserve, yesss. But sssomeone told Maliusss our location."

Broon's face was troubled.

Will piped up, wiping his sandy-colored face so darker streaks appeared where his tears had been. "I said the Watchers were not to be trusted. For months there have been rumors among the Mudgluck and the Quickwillow. Malius has been moving among them."

A few Quickwillow were still hovering near us, their lights dimmed, but they gave a small synchronous chime of agreement and Broon squinted at them.

"I haven't been listening," he said. "For this I am sorry."

"That dragon," I said. "It didn't eat us. Jack got in front of me and it could have killed us both. But it only made a noise."

"It was calling it's Master," said Jack. "It would have killed me in another moment, if it hadn't been for Lucius and Ember."

"And Malius?" I asked Broon. "Why didn't Malius kill me or take me?"

"I don't know, Thea." Broon admitted. "I imagine he was going to but changed his mind at the last moment. Perhaps he felt too exposed."

He doesn't look at Jack, but around at his brown-hooded men. "I think we should be off. This is my land, but we're near the outskirts of it and still too close to the boundaries for perfect safety."

With this he motioned for us to fall in behind him and we started our hike westward.

120

The men in the brown hoods followed us for a time, but all except the four carrying the Lady of Fire and the small turtle, soon slipped away in different directions, disappearing into the trees.

These were the Thornmen, so nicknamed because many of them were in hiding after having earned the ire of Stoneham in some way or another. They made their way to Broon's land and lived deep in the Thorn, defending the forest and its inhabitants, or entering the chasm and driving off Malius's soldiers or raiders.

They reminded me of the old tales of Robin Hood and his Merry Men. I half expected to see a man in a green hood come bounding out of the trees with Will Scarlett in tow. When I said this, only Broon looked as if he understood, while Jack, Will, and Dominus were puzzled.

"Who's Robin Hood?" asked Will.

I spent the better part of an hour telling them the stories I had read in school. Will liked it, but Jack drew his eyebrows together.

"A King who can't be bothered to stop fighting some silly war and come back and rule his kingdom?" he asked. "Why would anyone waste all their time defending that kind of ruler?"

"Because he was a good King," I said. "He didn't think his brother was going to tax his people so heavily."

But I agreed. What kind of King left their people to starve? Did no one tell him his brother was a terrible stand-in?

I thought about the Thornwoldian people. The men today had stared at me with quiet regard. When one came near me, he obsequiously bowed. I smiled at him but noted the gauntness of his face and the tired lines around his eyes.

These men had been fighting something terrible for twenty years. Dealing with fire-breathing dragons, and nearly indestructible soldiers and the loss of their homes and families. Waiting for someone to come and fix their situation.

They thought that person was me. All because my mother and father ran away. My father, the rightful King, had refused to return, but here I was. The daughter who had kept the family magic against all odds, and now I represented all of Thornwold's hopes.

I was troubled. If I couldn't do what they expected – and after seeing the dragon I knew what terrible danger I was walking into – how was I to look any of them in the face?

121

We had walked through deep forest and wide meadows, passed waterfalls and streams. Now we were headed steadily downhill. The forest had opened up into an enormous valley and the winding path we followed was taking us directly into the center of it. I couldn't see any house, but I hoped it was only because of the trees in our way.

A wooden bridge had been built over a small river, and as we crossed it, I came to an uncomfortable conclusion. If I were to continue on this dangerous journey, I was going to have to do it alone. I couldn't put Jack, Will, Dominus or Ironsides in further danger.

I felt fairly confident in my ability to throw magic spells and defend myself from those silent soldiers, but the enormous dragon was a different story. It would have eaten Jack in a moment if not for poor Lucius and brave Ember.

Ember's small, still form lying on a smoking field rose in front of my eyes. I thought about my terror at losing Ironsides and the blood on Dominus's neck.

I couldn't be responsible for any of them, I decided. At the first opportunity, I would slip away and head toward Stoneham. After all, I knew the rest of the plan. I knew Stoneham lay to the south. I would keep my eyes open in Broon's house and try to discreetly find out how to get out of the Thorn and to the chasm. Perhaps when everyone was asleep, I could get away.

I had a moment of discomfort, thinking about Jack's reaction when he learned I had gone. Would he be angry? I shoved the thought away and gritted my teeth. It didn't matter. This was my responsibility. My parents left this mess and it was up to me to clean it up.

I felt a small shift in the burden I carried. The resentment and bitterness I had developed in Brell lessened slightly. I had made a decision that was my own. No one had forced me into it. The action was significant, but I didn't know it.

I told myself that at least in Thornwold, I was needed. In Brell, I was only pushed into things I disliked or wasn't fit for. Here was something I was meant to do. A task belonging to me and me alone. It wasn't the university in Moor, but it was the next best thing.

Will gave a whoop of joy and I looked up, startled as the path we were on broadened and leveled out. There, in front of us, was Lilywell.

Great pools of water lay in faint golden light, dotted with enormous lilies in delicate shades of white and pink and a deeper purple. The golden paths between them were edged with tall rushes and soft cattails. Willow trees trailed their delicate branches in the water, while above us, the open sky deepened to an evening gold. Far away, across the interlacing paths and pools, home lights gleamed out.

Broon has lifted the knocker and let it fall once. The sharp crack of brass hitting brass echoes through the air around us and sends a sweet ringing through the house.

There is a pitter patter of small steps, and the great door swings silently open. A small man, no higher than my waist, stands aside to let us enter, bowing solemnly.

He has rather frog-like features. His bulbous eyes are set far apart. His mouth is wide, but it turns up in a welcoming smile. He is dressed in a soft leaf-colored robe and his feet are bare.

"Good evening, friends," he says, and his voice is rather croaky.

I picture him perched on a lily pad outside and have to stifle a giggle. Jack grins at me as if he knows what I'm thinking. Will, Dominus, and I all peer over the little man's head down a long, dim hall where soft torchlight winks over wood and stone.

"Come in, come in, to peace and safety!" says Broon, ushering the men carrying Ember and Iron first through the door, and then standing aside for the rest of us.

At these comforting words, we enter the house. Inside, Broon closes the door and makes a small signal with his right hand. The green-robed man disappears, only to return with two additional little men. They are also dressed in green and reminiscent of amphibian-like creatures. These pour wooden bowls of sweet wine for us. I sip mine gratefully and find my exhaustion dropping away as I drink.

Dominus, who had been looking less red and golden glorious and rather faded, appears stronger after a long draught of the drink. Jack drinks deeply from his and some color comes into his pale face.

The men have lowered Ember to the floor. Ironsides is still perched on her arm, his anxious eyes watching her quietly.

"There's nothing you can do for her right now, old friend," says Broon. He motions to me and I gently pick up Iron and put him on my shoulder. He doesn't protest.

Ember's face is serene and beautiful. Her sparkling red and gold tinted skin, so dim on the field, has regained some of its luster. She is still peacefully asleep. The men lift her and move down the hall, disappearing through a side door.

Jack, sipping from his bowl, glances up as Broon whispers a word to one of his green-robed servants. The little man scurries off.

"What's that about?"

"We must find out what we can about the Watchers. If they have betrayed us, we should know. For Lucius."

One of the small men, the one who has opened the door and is clearly in charge of the others, makes a startled movement.

"Yes, Pog." Broons says. "It's true, I'm sorry to say. Poor Lucius has fallen fighting one of Malius's evil manifestation dragons. He fought bravely and well, but even living silver —" He shakes his head.

The frog man looks glum, but Broon gestures to the rest of us. "See that our guests are well cared for. Baths for all and a meal is what we chiefly need!"

With this he strides away down the dark hall and disappears behind a large door at the end of it.

There is a tug on my tunic, and I look down. Pog is indicating I should follow him. Jack is slipping away after one of the other little men, giving me a sharp nod as a way of saying he will see me soon. Dominus has gone off his own way, looking as if he knows the house well. Will is following him. I trail after the small serving man as he leads me down a lengthy corridor.

Opening a door, he shows me into a large room. The room is entirely round. Round windows with round panes of glass are set here and there in the walls, not in any particular symmetry, but as if they have fitted themselves comfortably into the natural gaps in trees.

Over my head is a thick roof made of green, golden, and orange leaves, held in place by a woven net of thin branches. Beneath my feet, the floor is sanded smooth. There is a large bed in the center of the room growing from the floor. Rich, brown limbs grow in a rectangle and the branches entwine to create a sturdy canopy and bed frame. On this is a thick mattress and blankets. A vanity table is placed against one wall, fitting snugly into its curve.

On it are brushes and an assortment of perfume bottles and soaps. But my attention is drawn by the large wooden, claw footed bathtub with steaming hot water, the delicious, musky scent of sandalwood rising from it.

With a sigh, I strip off my torn and dirty clothes and drop them on the floor. I nearly throw myself into the hot water, my muscles screaming as waves of heat roll over me. I should be sleepy, but magically, the water wakes me up. There is a tingle on my hands. The liquid is healing any scratches or small cuts I have received over the last two days.

Iron plunges in beside me and climbs out, shaking himself like a little dog. He gives a stretch and collapses next to the tub on a small wooden stand with washcloths on it.

"Ironsides," I say, holding out a hand for him look at. "Is this water magic? Look!"

The turtle puts his head on one side as the last of faint scratches on my hands disappear.

"The water is from the magic well. It's a special treat for us. Broon doesn't allow just anyone to bath in the magic waters of the Lilywell."

He picks up one of his back feet. "I didn't like to mention it, but I had a small cut here this morning. It's gone now."

I give a stretch and plunge my whole head underwater. I spend some time washing my hair.

When I finally finish, which is difficult to do because unlike normal bathwater, the Lilywell water doesn't cool or lose its sweet-smelling soapy scent, I climb out carefully and find my torn and dirty clothes cleaned and mended and laid out for me on the bed. I comb my long hair out and leave it loose to dry.

"Another magical house," I muse to no one, as I put on my clothes. "I do like that part of this adventure."

Iron emerges from his shell, dry now and yawning hugely. "It is convenient," he agrees.

When I am dressed, I pick up Ironsides and put him on my shoulder. Together we open my door and head down the long hallway. Iron tells me what turns to take. It's clear he has been here many times.

Broon's dining hall is glowing with soft light and the faint sound of wooden chimes. The room is long and spacious. High windows set at uneven levels reflect the warm candlelight spilling over from lanterns. Elaborately carved wooden wind chimes hang among the roof branches, which stretch out from wall to wall. These shudder slightly in invisible breezes, their beautiful echoing sound making a strange song.

I sit at the long table and eat my supper in dreamy delight. Since setting my feet on the paths leading through the pools to Broon's beautiful front door, I had shed anxiety and worry. I felt more safe and secure than I had felt since leaving Brell.

Down the table from me, Jack leans back in his chair, conversing with Dominus in a soft tone. A large scratch on his face is healed and his hair flops over his eyes in the way that makes me want to push it back. I look away from him.

Ironsides has made his way over to Ember. She wears a loose dressing gown of silk. Her hair is long and loose. Her eyes are red from weeping, but she smiles and gives him a small pat. The two don't talk much, but Broon is sitting on the other side of Ember and keeps up a steady stream of low conversation.

I take a swallow of water from a wooden cup next to my plate. It must be Lilywell water because it buzzes in my throat in a curious way.

I try and keep my face composed as I think about leaving here and leaving all my companions behind. *Ironsides sleeps soundly enough* I think with a pang of regret. He might not understand I'm gone until I'm miles away. I have to be careful of my facial expressions. He has known me my whole life and can always tell when something is wrong.

Luckily, he is too preoccupied with Ember to pay much attention to me. I recall the flash of vision I had had when leaving the caverns, the image of a man with Ember. I resolve to ask him about it later when we are alone. After all, it might be the last time I have the chance.

"Are you finished, Thea?" Jack's voice cuts into my gloomy thoughts. He is staring at my face, making me flush. I hope he doesn't know what I am thinking. Not about Ember and Iron, but about leaving them all here.

"Yes, I think so." My plate is empty. The food is delicious, and I've eaten every scrap.

"Let me show you around," Jack says standing up and coming over to me. "I grew up here, you know."

"Okay," I agree, with a glance at Broon, who is smiling at me, and Iron, who gives an absent motion of his shell in my direction.

But Ember holds her hand out to me and I take it, holding it against my face. She has saved our lives. She and Lucius. I bend and kiss her on her warm, sparkling cheek. She'll be safe from me soon enough. They all will.

We set off, leaving Will and Dominus drinking merrily from wooden bowls of wine and beginning a game consisting of a flat board painted with squares and carved wooden figures. The goal appears to be to knock as many of the other players pieces down as possible.

"This way," says Jack, leading me down a long hall. "This is the library," he opens a door and shows me inside. The walls are lined with books and scrolls and I give a hop of delight.

I go over and take a book down from the shelf. It has a dull green cover. "A *History of Zenur*" I read aloud. "What's Zenur?"

"A country far away. I've only been there once. Sailing with Serafin."

"Won't you tell me about Serafin?" I ask. "You were going to, but we got interrupted by the dragon."

I blush and turn away, thinking about the moment in the forest, our faces close together. He might have kissed me if it weren't for the interruption.

Jack appears to be thinking the same thing, because he grins at me lazily and throws himself down in a velvet high-backed chair.

"Sure," he agrees. "If you tell me what you're planning."

I am stunned. "I'm not planning anything," I say quickly.

"Yes you are. I've been watching your face all day on the road here. You would look at Will or Dominus or Broon and then clench your jaw and look sad."

He leans back and cocks one eyebrow at me. "You are

planning something, and you need to tell me what it is."

"I am not planning anything," I insist. Trying to ignore the pang of delight that comes from knowing he has been watching me all day, I turn away from him and stare at the shelves in front of me.

"Thea, look at me."

Jack comes up behind me and I turn around to face him. His gray eyes stare into mine, searching. I decide a half-truth is best.

"Okay. I had planned to go on without you all. But now I realize it was a stupid idea and I wouldn't get far without help. That's what I was thinking about on the way here."

Jack glares down at me for a long moment. He is suspicious, but he accepts what I'm saying.

"Don't you dare leave this house without me," he says.

I stare at him, surprised by the anger in his voice and noting he hasn't said 'us' but 'me'.

It's his turn to flush. "You know what I mean. You need us. All of us." He turns away from me and rubs his head. "Just promise me you won't do anything silly."

"Okay," I lie.

I roll my eyes, but I'm smiling. I put the book back in its place on the shelf. "How about you show me the rest of this place?"

Jack goes to open the door. The instant his back is turned, I note the spot on the shelves where I'd seen it. Stacked high, are dusty covers of ancient books of maps. Some are in scrolls and some are leather-bound.

But one in particular: one is thin with a narrow binding, words carefully lettered on its spine in gold. A map of the chasm.

Broon's house is silent.

Jack and I had roamed the house until late in the evening. He had shown me the various rooms, including one with the magical well of Lilywell. The well was made of stone and had a wooden cover. Lifting the cover, one could see deep into crystal water. Taking a dipper, we both drank from it. As we did so, I felt my fears dissolve.

I can do this. Get the map and steal away from here on my own. Already I had noted a side door close to my room that led to the kitchens. From there another passage led out and down to the golden pools outside. Once I had the map, I could backtrack from the library, and grab some extra food on the way through the kitchens. It was going to be easy.

Saying goodnight to Jack outside my door, he again looked into my face carefully for any sign of deception, but I made my expression blank.

"Goodnight, Thea," he said softly.

He leaned his arm over my shoulder against the door behind me and his soft eyes traced my lips. For an instant, I wavered. But the image of the dragon rose in front of me and I lifted my chin resolutely. I wouldn't be responsible for something happening to him.

"Goodnight, Jack," I said firmly, even as he bent his head toward mine. I ducked under his arm and went into my room and shut the door in his puzzled face.

It wasn't that I didn't want him to kiss me, but I worried if he did all my resolve to leave would go to pieces. I regretted not being able to say goodbye to Dominus and Will, but I hoped they would understand.

I looked around for Ironsides, but he wasn't there. He must still be talking to Broon and Ember. I left the door slightly open for him and crawled in bed, telling myself I would only sleep for a few hours.

Miraculously, I do manage to wake while the house is still dark. The night outside is turning from a deep black to a dark gray. It is time to go. Ironsides is still not there and I glance around, uncertain.

Perhaps he had been given his own room or is still closeted with Broon and Ember, or as was his habit when we lived in Brell, merely fallen asleep wherever he lay. I am guilty that I won't see him before I leave. He's going to be terribly upset.

I gather my pack and make sure I still have my Mama's things. My Mama's necklace is hanging over the edge of the tub, where I had left it while I was washing my hair.

I pick it up and turn it over in the lessening gloom. It still shines beautifully. The faint light catches the lavender glass of the

'S' and it sparkles. I drop it over my head and experience its familiar, comforting buzz.

I have to get into the library and then back out through the kitchens. Softly as I can, I pull the door wide and creep out into the hallway which is still half-lit with low burning torches. I make my way down the long hall and find the library door. Relieved to find it half open, I go inside and shut it behind me. A small lantern is still burning here, low.

Crossing the room swiftly, I grab the thin leather-bound book holding the chasm map. Scanning the rest of the maps is the work of a moment. There are no maps of Stoneham, and I shake off a twinge of disappointment. Once I'm there, I'll just have to figure it out.

As I turn back to leave, I nearly jump out of my skin.

"Hello, Thea," smiles Broon, his white teeth glowing evenly in the shadows.

"And where are you headed?" demands Ironsides, perched on the arm of the chair next to him.

"Nowhere," I stammer. "I was looking for something to read." Even as I say it, Broon and Iron look pointedly at my pack.

"Fully dressed already?" snaps the turtle. "Since when are you an early riser?"

I sigh sulkily, but Broon laughs at me. "Nothing happens in this house of which I am not fully aware, Thea."

He says this gently enough, but I am reminded of the first time we met and the obvious power radiating off him in strands.

As if to demonstrate this, he casually flicks a hand toward the door, and it closes with a click. He motions again and there is an insistent bump behind my knees. Another velvet armchair has made its way over to me and is pushing my legs gently.

I think of simply walking out but decide against it. Broon would catch me in a minute if I were to run. I sit down with an exasperated thump.

"Now," Broon leans forward with his hands held in front of him prayer-like, his fingertips touching. "Where are you going?"

"To Stoneham," I mutter, knowing its best to confess. I look up at him and am surprised his eyes are not accusing, merely neutral pools of brown.

"I need to do this alone."

"Why?" asks Iron, still angry.

"Because of what happened in the forest. I nearly lost you, Iron."

And I can't bear the thought of it because you are all I have left of my parents and my life before I want to finish, but don't. There are tears in my eyes.

"Dominus got hurt. Jack was nearly eaten by a dragon. Ember fell hundreds of feet and Lucius was pulverized! Will was fine this time, but who knows about next time? You're all risking yourselves and it's clear Malius only wants me. He'll kill all of you to get to me."

"Oh Thea," says Ironsides, sounding less angry. "You don't need to be noble. We all know the risk we're taking."

Broon holds up a finger. "Except I agree with Thea, Iron" he interjects.

We both stare at him.

"No, Broon," sputters Iron. "I won't allow it. She's a child."

"*She's* nearly seventeen," I say grumpily. The dark gray outside is getting lighter. I shift in my chair.

Broon guesses my thoughts. "This will only take a few minutes, Thea."

He turns to the turtle with a benign expression. "Let me explain," he says hopefully, but the turtle has withdrawn into his shell in a huff.

Broon grins at me and taps Ironsides shell. "Listen," he coaxes. "Thea can take you with her."

I start to object, but Broon interrupts. "You will take Iron with you, or you will go back to bed now, and tomorrow you will explain to Dominus, Will and Jack that you must leave them behind. I know Mudglucks. Stubborn race. I know my adopted sons. They won't let you leave without them. This is my bargain."

He has said *sons*. I remember the way Jack cradled Dominus's bleeding head in his arms, calling him *brother*. I try to glare at Broon but can't quite manage it. He's right and I am defeated.

Iron's head has emerged.

"I have had a vision," says Broon.

"A vision concerning what?" Iron's scornful tone tells me he doesn't particularly hold with visions.

"A vision of Jack's death."

I gasp. Iron is troubled, but he falls silent.

"If he continues with you, I have seen his death."

I thought you said visions aren't dependable," I say, forgetting I don't want Jack or any of them to come with me. "You said they don't always show the truth."

Broon is pleased. "You have a good memory. Yes, its true visions are often shown to us as mere interpretations of our own fears or to give us a hint about the direction of our fates. But this was different. It came to me in a Sending from the Dark Mountain."

Ironsides gasps this time.

"Ironsides understands what a Sending from the Monks of Dark Mountain means."

I stare from the turtle to the giant man curiously. "Why? What does a Sending mean? What's a Sending?"

"It's a special kind of message between magic folk," says Iron stiffly. I can tell he doesn't want to say more, but I press him anyway.

"What kind of special message? Involving Jack? Why?"

"The Monks of Dark Mountain are old and very wise. For centuries they have practiced the magical arts. They are skilled in scrying and in times of crisis they use their power to warn us of what may come."

Broon explains all this in a thoughtful tone, as if he is thinking of other warnings, other times.

"So it may not come? The vision you saw?"

"It may not. But the Monks have a history of being accurate more often than not. Besides," he stretches tiredly. "Their leader, Monk Wulfsiege, owes me a favor."

Ironsides is silent.

"Well," I stand up. "It's settled. Jack should not come."

Or the rest of them I think.

"Yes," Broon says, "but you must take Iron with you. I have foreseen a role for him to play."

"What sort of role?" asks Iron. "I don't trust visions."

But Broon only taps his shell gently. "You'll find out, my old friend." There is a note of sorrow in Broon's voice. It makes me uneasy.

"What am I missing here? What's going to happen to

Ironsides?" I shake my head. "I won't take him along if something —" But the turtle stops me.

"No, no, Thea," he says. "It's not how these things work."

He exhales grimly at Broon. "As I well know."

There is a small silence, while we three consider this. Ironsides shakes himself out of it first with a touch of his old impatience.

"Then let's be off. Thea, get to the kitchens and get us some food that will travel. Get enough for two or three days."

Startled by his sudden shift in mood, I do what he says. When I come back, Broon is putting a vial of water into my traveling pack.

"Some Lilywell water," he says, and then adds some fire stones. "For warmth in the chasm. It gets cold down there at night."

He takes out a small scroll and adds it to my pack. "A copy of the map of Stoneham's passageways. We can't have you getting lost inside the castle. Even if you do, a map is useful."

He grins at me, white teeth in his dark face. I am not comforted, but Iron gives a short bark of a laugh.

I pack the food, while Iron insists on looking at and approving each item.

Broon embraces me briefly. I am crushed in his enormous arms. He puts Iron on my shoulder, with a laugh at the indignant look on the turtle's face as he's lifted through the air.

"He's never let me do it," murmurs Broon to me. "It might be my last chance."

I don't want to consider what he means.

"Ironsides will guide you to the chasm's edge. After that, use the map. I've marked the right way."

I open the map book he hands to me and note the fine silver line gleaming along the twists and turns of the cavern.

"Thank you, Broon" I manage.

"Bless you, child," says Broon, placing his hand on my hair. "I'm sorry this task falls to you. But I am hopeful for the future."

Iron manages a smile for Broon. His small body is quivering slightly.

"Goodbye, my old friend." he says. "Give Ember my love."

Broon lays one finger on the turtle's shell and leaves it there. "I am also hopeful that you will soon be back to give it to her yourself."

We go out the side kitchen door and follow the golden paths through the pools of water, silver and rose in the growing light of morning. As we reach the edge of the forest, Iron nuzzles the side of my face.

"We go south, Thea," he says in a low voice.

I turn and gaze back at Broon's house. It is solid and beautiful among its lily pools and cascading waterfalls. It's wooden walls amplify peace and safety. I wonder if I will ever see it again.

But I think of Jack and clench my jaw. Turning south, I plunge into the thick trees and disappear.

CHASM

As we go through the thick trees, and leave the safety of Broon's lands, the forest reminds me of my first day in it.

The trees are enormous, taking minutes to walk around them, and the rising sun shines faintly green and golden. The path through the trees is clear, and the tangle of undergrowth only winds itself about the roots and does not cross our way.

The colorful lights of the Quickwillow hover above us, though none of them lead me, as they had before, but only quiver in the air as I walk by, swooping and making loops, and zipping off on business of their own. If we hadn't been headed to an enormous chasm and certain demise, I would enjoy the cool, quiet walk through this enchanted place.

The eyes of the Watchers are nowhere to be found. I am grateful for this because means they are not following us. Whether this is because they haven't noticed us yet, or don't find us to be a threat, I'm not sure.

Iron shifts on my shoulder.

"It's not far now," he says. He has been unusually quiet since we left Lilywell.

"Good," I say. "The further away we are from Lilywell, the better."

"I don't think Broon will allow the others to come after us," he says reading my unspoken words correctly. "Jack will try, of course, but Broon is good at helping people see reason."

His voice is rueful. It reminds me of the odd conversation between them in the library.

"What was all that, Iron? What did Broon mean about you

"having a task"?"

Iron is silent for so long, I wonder if he has heard me, but then he speaks. "It was to do with the story of my life. Of my debt owed to your family."

"To my family?" I say blankly. What could a turtle possibly owe to a human? I don't want to offend Ironsides, so I say instead, "You've always been in our family. Ember told me so."

"Yes. I've always been in your family. At least, in this form."

For a moment, the words don't register.

The golden lines on his shell are gleaming in the touches of morning sun slanting through leaves. His old dew-bright eyes are sunken in his wrinkled face. If turtles could shrug, he might have. Instead he closes his eyes and appears pained.

"Iron! You don't mean to say you are not – not a –" I falter, unsure how to word this particular revelation.

"Not a turtle?" Iron says mildly. "No, I am not a turtle."

I stop and lift him down from my shoulder, depositing him on a convenient stump. I sit down on the ground in front of him, so we are face to face.

"Ironsides. I'm not going another step until you tell me what you are."

But Iron shakes his head uneasily, "It isn't anything to get excited about, Thea." He frowns darkly at the moss beneath his clawed feet and hesitates.

"I have to know, Iron," I insist. "If you are enchanted, what do we need to do to fix it?"

He snorts appreciatively at this. "Always eager to help. It's exactly what your mother and father said when they found out. I am always stunned at the unfailing kindness of your family."

"But surely you didn't do anything terrible. Iron, I know you. You couldn't do anything bad."

"Don't say that until you've heard the whole story, and don't interrupt me until I've finished."

I am nervous, but I sit back and wait.

"I am merely an enchanted man. A monk of the Dark Mountains, to be exact. My father was a harsh man who disliked my penchant for adventuring and wanted me to stay home. Since I was the eldest and marked for leadership, it was expected that I should be silent and wise. That I should care more about books and ancient records than riding off the mountains and exploring the plains and valleys around us. It was expected, too, I should marry a kinswomen of mine, a woman of the Light Mountains. I was not to ride off to the caverns and meet and fall in love with the daughter of the Lady of Fire and she with me."

I gasp in comprehension. "Ember?"

But Iron is still speaking bitterly. "It wasn't done. All the things I did. But I was young and wanted to live my life, not the life someone had in mind for me."

I feel a pang. I know something about this story.

"One day," he goes on. "I went too far. I had yet another argument with my parents over my future. I tore out of the gates of the Dark Mountain City in anger. In a ravine, I came across a lost young man who sought information only the Dark Monks possessed. I knew it was wrong, but I showed him the secret libraries and the sacred spaces and gave him access to a certain book. One showing the way into the underground passages of Stoneham — and the secret way to an ancient magical object."

I stare at him in horror. "Oh, Iron," I breathe. "You didn't."

Iron gazes at me with his eyes full of shame. "I was so angry, Thea. I was so young. Why shouldn't this young man get what he wanted? I never could have what I wanted."

He swallowed something and rasped, "It was wrong. I knew it was wrong, but I did it anyway."

Tears prick my eyes. Ironsides had given Malius a path to steal my family's magic. A way to steal my family's throne. He was the reason they had fled to Brell. The reason I was now forced into this situation. I want to howl at the unfairness of things.

"And your father? He turned you into this," I gesture at his small form.

"Yes." Iron says tonelessly. "'To remain a turtle until I have earned back what I gave away. I made my way into your family and have remained with them ever since. I must make things right, but I'm not sure how to do it."

I drop my head into my hands and cry. For myself. For my Mama and Papa and for Ironsides, too. For what an unholy mess people make of things.

On his stump, Ironsides moves anxiously.

"Thea," he says in a voice I have never heard him use before.

Soft. Pleading.

"Your parents knew. They forgave me. They tried to help me. They entrusted you to my care the day you were born. I've been a watchdog over you. But, Thea," he swallows something, "I understand if you can't forgive me. You can leave me behind if you want. You must be angry with me. It's all my fault. Everything is my fault."

I don't hesitate.

"No, no," I say, wiping my eyes with a dirty hand. "I'm sorry, Iron. It isn't your fault. You were angry. You weren't being treated fairly. You didn't know Malius was there to steal something. Anyway," I end grimly, "I understand how it is to be forced into a life you don't want. Of course, I forgive you. Don't worry."

With this, I give another shaky sob and take him and put him back on my shoulder, giving his rough shell a pat. He leans his small head on my cheek. His own eyes are wet.

"We are two of a kind, Thea," he says. "I only hope both of us can get what we want in the end."

I pat his shell again. "Ember has waited for you all this time?"

Iron is embarrassed but pleased.

"She has," he says gruffly, "but I have told her to go and find someone else if she can."

"She wouldn't," I say wisely.

We make our way to the edge of the forest of Thornwold by mid-afternoon. As we emerge from the trees, I see it. At my feet, uneven stairs disappear into it, leading straight down. There are no twists or turns.

"Iron," I whisper. "My God."

I am at a loss for words. I knew the chasm was an abyss. I knew it was huge. But I didn't comprehend how deep it was. It is a yawning crack in the earth. The bottom is miles away.

Far away, across the deep cleft filled to the brim with the tops of rock formations and slow drifting clouds, stands Stoneham. It's small in the distance, but a glowing beacon of light and beauty. I catch my breath as I look at my first home.

Iron is quiet on my shoulder. "It's been so long," he says. "I'd forgotten how beautiful it is."

Because it is beautiful. I had been thinking of it as a dark, wicked looking place, but it's walls are a warm, earth colored stone, and even though it is far away, I can make out the high turrets built in different styles. One is straight and slim, another rounded and curving, each with graceful parapet walks between them. The colored-glass windows set in the walls of the chapel catch the light and gleam in the sun.

Beyond it are two tall mountain peaks. One is nearer, with a cap of white, its blue curves and peaks shielding its smaller twin sister. All around the castle lies a flat white plain. Several roads weave through this.

Just below the castle, are the remains of what looks like a ruined city. Even from this distance, I can see it is abandoned and many of its buildings are broken shells.

"No one lives in the city then?" I ask Iron, who shakes his head sadly.

"Stoneham was more than just a castle, Thea. It was a thriving place with theaters and tradesmen and alehouses. There were markets and gardens and hundreds of people who lived there. It was diverse and prosperous."

Something about the empty buildings of the ruined city makes me shiver, but I nod, and then look at the castle again.

It is a fairytale castle. I had no trouble imagining it covered in roses, a sleeping princess in the tower. But, as I remind myself, I am the princess of this particular fairytale and wide awake. I am also dirty and hot after hours of walking through the Thorn and in need of a bath. I laugh at this thought and Iron eyes me nervously.

"Are you all right, Thea?" he asks, clearly concerned for my mental state.

"It's all right. I can't believe I ever lived there. It's so lovely."

Iron nuzzles his head on my cheek. "And it's yours," he says simply, "by rights."

I hadn't even thought of this. My own home. Such a home!

"Yes," I say, smiling a bit grimly and shouldering my pack. "Hang on then. Let's go and take it back."

With this bravado and without even a glance behind me, I begin the steep descent into the chasm.

It goes on and on. My legs begin to scream with pain as we walk down and down. We disappear into the cloud cover and soon emerge, dripping wet. Strange winds of pelting dirt attack my small frame.

Without asking his permission, I pluck Iron from my neck, where his claws are digging in uncomfortably, and deposit him none too gently into my pocket. At least one of us is out of the shelling dirt and glaring sun.

When the stairs finally end, I stumble forward, my legs giving way as we reach a flat level surface. The skin on my knees tears open. Bleeding, I move to a sitting position and bend my head, trying to stop it spinning.

We are deep in the chasm now. Sounds are odd and muted. There is no wind. We are too deep even for a breeze. It makes the air muffled and hot. The afternoon sun bakes the floor.

I drag myself over to the rocky wall and into the shade where the air is cooler. I dig in my pack and take out the bottle of Lilywell water. First, I drink deep. I pour some over my knees. The skin knits itself and the bleeding stops, but the area is still tender.

I dig out Ironsides, who is dizzy and sleepy. I pour him a capful of water and sprinkle some over his shell. He immediately appears better and more alert. We say nothing. We sit in the shade drinking water and breathing deep, trying to get used to the oppressive feel of the bottom of the world.

I take out the map book Broon gave us. The lines of silver show the end of the stairs and the winding way through the twists and turns of the chasm. It appears simple. Broon has given us the most direct route.

"So we can go straight for a ways," I say to Iron, "and we take two, no, three lefts."

"It shouldn't take us more than a day or so for us to reach the other side," he says, sounding raspy. He sneezes, blowing dust from his mouth. "Provided we don't run into trouble."

The chasm is silent and still.

"With all this rock," I say nervously, "we'll be sure to hear the echo of footsteps before we see them. So it's a good thing."

"Keep your eyes out for hiding spots," Iron cautions. "Just in case."

I shake away the thought of Malius's soldiers or one of his dragons and study the map. The silver lines go left three times and swerve to the right. I try and memorize this as I get to my feet. Setting Iron on my shoulder, I give him a pat. It's hard to not think of him as my pet and remember he's a man.

"Sorry about shoving you in my pocket. I was worried you'd fall off. It would have been the end of us both because I would have went diving after you."

"I was glad you did. I was having a devil of time hanging on," he coughs, releasing another small cloud. "But your pocket got filled with dust and that wasn't the best experience either. Let's hope the other set of stairs isn't so windy."

I groan, thinking of having to climb out of this hole. Going up is going to be much worse. We set off. At first it's easy enough. Then we pass a particularly large outcropping of rock and it cracks, sending a trail of dirt and dust and small boulders into the canyon. I sprint forward in a panic and skid to a stop when I realize it is only a small slide.

"Yes, those," mutters Ironsides. "The chasm is full of unstable rock formations, so be careful."

We pass more slides. Some are old and some have taken place recently. To avoid new ones, I learn to navigate. If I hear a small plink of scattered stones, I find its source. Sometimes the rattle and the accompanying shower of stones is close to us, sometimes its off down another passageway. Either way, it means get out of there in a hurry because boulders and dirt and rocks can come crashing down at any moment.

The worst part is the silence. At least the slides provide a noise and something to actively avoid. The silence is harsh and heavy. I long for the noises of the Thorn, birdsong, and sunlight slanting through leaves, growing grass and bubbling water. This hush of dust and rock is unsettling and unnatural.

We pass the first corpse. There isn't much of a body left. Only a skeleton and some dried bits I don't want to think about too much. It has been laying there for many years.

I stop and look at it. Nothing about it is familiar but, "Iron," I whisper, "do you think my Papa made it here?"

It's the first time I have mentioned him to anyone in

141

Thornwold.

"I was wondering if you'd been thinking about it," Iron admits. "I wondered it myself."

He looks at the body too. We are both quiet. There's no way to tell if it's my Papa. We walk on.

"Maybe it's better if he died without getting back here. Ember said the spells she and Broon used on the area nearest Brell were thick and confusing. She didn't think anyone could have made it through them without help."

Iron is silent and reflective. "I think if he had made it back to Thornwold," he finally says, "Broon and Ember would have told you. Even if the truth was painful." He glances back at the skeletal remains. "Thea —"

But he stops because we both hear it at the same time. The unified stomp of marching boots. It echoes faintly around the walls of the chasm. It's impossible to tell where its coming from, except it's getting louder and nearer. I freeze, listening.

"This way," says Iron after a moment. He motions to the left. "It's coming from down there."

I don't need to be told twice. Ordering the turtle to hang on tight, I dash away from the storm of marching feet, forgetting the path. I run until the noise fades, and then scramble to a stop and listen. The footsteps are faint, but again, they are growing louder.

"They are coming after us," I am starting to panic. "What should we do?"

Iron doesn't hesitate. "Find a place to hide," he says. "But get going!"

Before I can move, from up ahead there is another sound. The sound of more marching feet. There are two companies of soldiers and they are both headed in our direction. I back up, terrified.

"This way," cries Iron, motioning to my left. I sprint down another side passageway and keep going. I run for what feels like an hour, but really it is only minutes.

I take a left here, a right there. I am getting us hopelessly lost, but it doesn't matter. Behind us, the sound of the stomp of soldiers grows louder as we dodge our way through the flat, hot passageways of the canyon.

At last we come to a stop. Ahead of us is a solid wall. We are trapped. I dash to end of the wall, looking around for a way through or a boulder to hide behind, but it's no use. Malius's soldiers have trapped us and there too many of them. I think of the last time I faced them and wish desperately for enormous trees to drag them under the earth.

The earth! There is a rocky outcrop on either side of the nearly circular dead end. I have an idea. A dangerous, stupid idea.

"Hold on, Iron!" I yell.

Around the bend comes a company of large empty shells of armor, marching stonily in unison. There are at least four dozen of them. They come on and on. I wait, standing in the center of the passageway, rocky walls all around us.

One hundred yards, fifty yards, ten. Concentrating, I fling out my hands to either side of me and throw two shining blue jets of flame at each side of the passage. Two enormous rockslides begin as my magic hits the walls. The slides come shooting toward Malius's soldiers, growing stronger and gathering speed as they hit the wall of marching armor. Malius's men go crashing into each other as rock and mountains of dirt roll over them.

A split second later, I recognize that Iron and I are in danger of being dragged beneath it too. I leap backward as boulders come barreling toward us. Undaunted, I fling my hands out and hit the tops of the canyon walls again. I need more rock, more stones, more rolling waves of earth.

Iron yells at me to stop, but I don't. Another blue flame sends another rockslide. This one rolls over the first and Malius's soldiers are drowning in it. They make no noise, but their armor is clanking and ripping apart. I am backed up against the passageway wall, as far as I can get from the falling cliffs.

I cover my head and crouch low as slide after slide falls around us. The dust cloud is enormous, choking us. I cover Iron and I with my cloak and pray a rock doesn't crush us.

After a time, it all falls silent. I peer out, blinking in the aftermath. We are entirely enclosed on all sides with boulders and dirt and fallen walls. In a neat u-shape around us, the floor is clear of debris.

I give a whoop. "Look, Iron! We did it!"

"We?" sputters Ironsides, clambering out from under my cloak and choking on dust. "Thea, we could have been killed!"

"But we weren't!" I say. "The soldiers are all gone or stuck on the other side." I motion to the mountain in front of us. "There's no way they're getting through!"

Iron is shaking himself, emptying dirt out from his shell. "But we aren't getting out of here either," he points out.

He's right of course, but I am too exhilarated by my single-handed destruction of dozens of magical soldiers to admit I may have trapped us permanently. The rock walls have fallen in such a way, there isn't much chance of climbing out. They lay around us, nearly vertical.

"Perhaps when the dust settles some more I can think of something."

"Well, don't go blasting it again. At least, not without discussing it first."

I open my lips to retort there isn't time for discussion when one is being mown down by nearly indestructible soldiers, when there is a howl of twisting wind.

It bursts into our small circle, blowing my cloak free of dirt. Ironsides is knocked off my shoulder and into a pile of rocks. He lays on his back, struggling. I cover my head as my hair, freed from its braids, whips around my face, blinding me.

As quickly, the wind vanishes, and a tall figure emerges from the cloud of dust. Malius stands in front of me.

"That was settling," I say dryly. "The dust. You've whipped it up again."

I find I am not as frightened as I should be. I step back, careful to step in front of Iron's small form, as Malius towers over me. The bright green, smoky rimmed color is rolling off him in angry waves. It comes toward me, but I reach out, confident, and flick it away before it can envelope me.

Malius's eyes widen and the color disappears. "You've gained some control over your ability."

His voice sneers a bit on the last word, as if he doesn't think much of my magical prowess, but a tiny bit of orangish yellow creeps out of his body. Fear. Nervousness.

I decide the best way to cope with him is to be direct.

"What is it you want, Malius?"

"I should be asking you the same thing," he says. "What is it you want, Althea Morgan?"

His question is loaded. He doesn't mean the Globe or his defeat or the throne of Stoneham. He is asking me a much deeper question.

The confusion must show on my face because he laughs. His laugh makes me angry. The urge to tell him its none of his business what I want is on my tongue, but I have enough sense to say nothing.

He moves around me to sit down on a nearby rock. This relaxation of a battle stance startles me. I turn to face him, not willing to give up my position of shielding Ironsides. Behind me, Iron has managed to right himself. He is scampering off the pile of rocks.

"You want to be rid of this entire business. I can give you a way out if you like. I can give myself a way out, too."

He doesn't sound angry. His voice is interested and his frame watchful. I don't know how to respond.

"What do you mean?" I ask him carefully. "You'll give up the throne and —"

He laughs again and I fall silent.

"No, of course not." He gazes at nothing with a strange expression. "I will never give up Stoneham. Stoneham and Thornwold are mine. Once I decide something is mine, it's mine forever."

His eyes are feverishly bright as he looks at me. The strange bright green hue begins to trickle out of him, but as soon as I see it, it disappears as if it has never been. With a sharp intake of breath I understand something. He won't give up unless I kill him.

I haven't considered the real possibility of killing another person and what it means until right now. Killing empty armor, even armor enchanted to march and destroy, is not the same as killing a person with flesh and blood, a person with life experiences, thoughts, and feelings.

All this flashes through my mind. It must show in my own color, oozing out of me, because Malius is watching me speculatively. He can see the fear and I know it. He knows I know it.

"You are not up to it," is all he says.

There is something in his voice. It is too precise, too even. He is trying to hide something from me, but I'm not sure what it is.

"Let me offer you an alternative."

"What alternative?"

Malius gestures with his hand and the air turns into a shining oval surface. A mirror, but instead of reflecting us, it shows a scene.

The university in Moor spreads out in front of me. Students sit on stone benches, talking and laughing. Fountains sparkle in the beautiful grounds. Magnificent buildings surround them. Through a window in one of these are shelves filled with hundreds of books. I lean closer, fascinated despite myself.

"I can give you all this, Thea," says Malius. "All you have to do is say yes. I can send you home. You can pursue your dreams. Your friends in Brell will be nearby whenever you want to visit. Look!"

He gestures again and the scene changes. Abigail is teaching a young, fair-haired girl how to create a simple potion. The girl smiles and laughs, enjoying the work.

"Maggie and Thomas's daughter in future years," says Malius. "She has a natural gift for healing potions. Abigail will live to find the perfect apprentice to pass on her knowledge to, but she will always consider you her child."

Malius's voice is soothing and musical.

My eyes prick with tears. "She won't be upset with me?"

"Not at all, Thea. You will have an exciting career and travel to distant places."

Malius waves his beautiful fingers once more. Tall ships, sailing out on flat blue waters. I am tiny, my red hair pulled back, looking ahead to the far horizon.

"The perfect, happy, life. All you want."

The scene fades and disappears. The shimmer in the air vanishes. Rocky walls surround us.

"Or" says Malius, motioning around at the chasm, "You may choose a tomb. It's up to you."

I open my lips. I want to burst into tears and beg him to send me home, but there is a tiny sound behind me. Iron. It's the sound of his angry sputtering when he's so furious he doesn't know what to say. I whirl and stare at Ironsides. He is glaring at Malius. His small form is tense with rage and pain.

I gaze down at him. My oldest friend. My only friend at times.

An enchanted man dependent on me to do the right thing. To help him. All that is left of my family. My family.

I know what it is I truly want.

Stooping slowly, watching Malius out of one eye, I pick up the turtle and place him on my shoulder. He clings there, his claws digging in. I turn and face Malius.

"No, Malius," I say levelly. I take a step forward and raise my hand as if to throw one of my streaks of blue flame directly at his heart. "No thank you. I don't think I'll choose either. I think I'll take Thornwold – if you please."

Malius face twists in fury. He moves toward me, and I dodge backward, throwing a searing wall of white light around myself and Iron. Malius's hand touches it and I can smell the burning flesh. He yelps in pain and stumbles back from me. We stare at each other through my net of protective white fire and his angry face dissolves into a strange smile, into a blast of hot wind throwing me to the ground, and he is gone.

Rescue

After Malius disappears, I roll over wearily and sit up. I pick up Iron from where he has landed and hold him on my outstretched palms. I look at him in the face.

"Oh, Iron," I say, and the tears come. "Thank you."

Iron is tearful as well. "I thought you might say yes, Thea." He gives a small sob. "I thought you might leave me here. There was nothing I could do to stop you."

"But you did it. You reminded me of your presence. You reminded me of who I am. In the future, keep reminding me."

Iron bends his head and rubs my palm with his cheek.

I wipe my face. "But oh Iron," I whisper. "How am I ever going to kill him? He was right. I don't think I can do it. I'm not a murderer."

Iron makes the full body hop reminding me of a person's shrug. "The plan was never to kill him," he says, trying to sound comforting. "Perhaps you won't have to."

But he is wrong. I had seen it in Malius's eyes. Only death would stop him.

"He was right about this," I gesture around. "We are in a tomb."

The sun is setting. As deep as we are, the light has gone from the hole we are in. It's getting darker and darker. I make a fire from the fire stones. The glow rises and creates shadows on the high walls. The images flicker upward.

Iron looks uneasily around at the moving shadows. "Isn't it rather like a beacon?"

"It doesn't matter. Malius knows where we are."

We are both thinking of the large black dragon. If a dragon finds us here, one blast of fiery breath will destroy us instantly.

I give the turtle's shell a pat. "We should try and get some sleep. Tomorrow we can figure out a way out of here."

If there is a way I think gloomily.

Iron is quiet. I take out some food and we eat a little, drinking some of the Lilywell water. It refreshes us both. I am exhausted. I wrap myself in my cloak and stretch out on the rocky ground. Iron curls up in the crook of my elbow, withdrawing his head and feet into his shell. We both fall into an uneasy sleep.

Somewhere on the earth the sun has risen. Our prison is still enclosing us, but the chasm is growing lighter. I am awakened by a rumble and a crash. A large boulder has sprung from the largest rockslide and landed fifty feet away from where we are sitting. Irons head emerges.

"What was it?" he groans. His eyes widen as he sees the boulder.

"I don't know."

I stand up and walk carefully toward the boulder. Before I can reach it, another boulder from the slide shoots straight up into the air and lands next to the first with an enormous sound. Someone or something is digging through to us from the other side.

I stumble backward, grabbing both Iron and my pack. I sprint toward the wall farthest away from the slide and cower against it, holding Ironsides tightly against me. Boulders are thundering down the heap of slides. Falling dirt and rock make clouds of dust. The noise is tremendous. There is final burst of loose earth and I duck my head. Silence falls around us.

"Thea!" says Iron, who has squirmed away from my hands to have a look at the situation.

I lift my head and squint through the hazy air. Emerging from the large hole he has made in the rockslide and looking pleased, is Will. I start to laugh and stand up, perching Ironsides on my shoulder.

"Will!" I am so glad to see him I am dizzy. Behind him,

through the low opening slides Dominus, red and golden. Beyond this, comes Jack dirty and worse for wear, but grinning.

I rush toward them, stooping to hug Will and run my fingers down Dominus's neck. I turn to Jack.

"Thought you two might need some help," he says.

I throw my arms around him nearly knocking him off his feet.

"Did Broon send you?" I ask, releasing him and noticing he's flushed and flustered.

"He didn't," Jack says, trying to regain his composure. "He doesn't know. But if he thinks I was going to walk off and let you go through this chasm alone —"

"Wait, wait," I interrupt him, frowning now. "Broon doesn't know? Where does he think you are?"

"What does it matter, Thea?" he snaps. "You clearly need our help. I can't believe you ran off and left us!"

His voice is condescending, and it irks me. After all, I had successfully fought off dozens of Malius's soldiers and even managed to wound Malius without Jack's help.

"For your information," I say coldly, "I didn't run off. Broon agreed with me that I needed to do this alone."

"And that I should be here, too," Iron reminds me grumpily, nudging my chin. I ignore him.

Jack is angry too, but Dominus slides smoothly between us. "Children, children, it'sss all right. We have ressscued you and now we can all go together to Ssstoneham. The more of usss there are, the sssafer we will be."

I am shaking my head. "No!"

In my head, I can hear Broon's voice, *Jack will die if he continues with you.* I am not going to let it happen.

Jack turns on me, jaw set and eyes flashing. "Thea, I'm not hearing any arguments. You can't make it through this alone. Even with Ironsides. I'm not letting you go to Stoneham alone and I'm not letting you —"

This is too much.

"You are going to die!" I blurt. "Broon had a vision of your death if you come with me. Do you think I'm going to let that happen?"

Jack turns pale. Dominus's drops his enormous head and stares at me. Iron moves uneasily. It's Will who breaks the silence.

"Visions aren't always true, Thea." His voice is small and uncertain.

"I don't care. I'm not going to risk it. I'm not going to let any of you risk it."

I turn to Will. "Thank you for rescuing us. Really. We needed help. We are fine now, and Iron and I are going on alone."

I am pleading with all of them.

"But Will's right, Thea," Ironsides says reluctantly. "We did get ourselves into a fix. We wouldn't have gotten out of it without help. Not to mention, we are hopelessly lost, even if we are now free."

I am beyond frustrated. Broon had agreed with me. Without the giant man's support now, I am going to be overruled.

But Dominus is watching Jack's face.

"I don't know Ironsssides," he says slowly, "I won't risssk Jack'sss life either. If Broon sssaid it wasssn't a good idea – I'm not sssure –"

Jack is glaring at all of us, ready to explode, his whole body shaking.

"Broon is always having visions," he snarls. "How many of those have come true? Visions of your mother taking back the throne. It wasn't her; it was you. Visions of me killing my father. Broon decides it can't happen that way. Visions don't matter because with a wave of his powerful hand, he decides to change their meaning. With a council meeting, they change a person's fate!"

His face is twisted with pain and anger. Dominus closes his eyes wearily and Will is horrified. I stare at Jack, a new idea dawning on me.

"You want to kill Malius. You want it to be you. This isn't about me at all."

Jack whirls on me in a rage, "That's not true, Thea!" he bellows, "That's not what I mean! Broon – I – I – they've ruined everything!"

He falters and I know I'm right.

Jack wants revenge. He doesn't care about me, but he does want to be the hero of this story. I understand the gray green waves of pain and sadness coming off him when we first met. He wants vengeance and the glory, and I am in his way.

I think of the way he tried to kiss me. How he confided in me the story of his parentage. How I thought he cared for me.

Jack has fallen silent. The anger has faded out of him as he stares at my face, realizing I know the truth. No one says a word. Then he bows to me stiffly.

"Your Highness," he says. His voice is quiet and defeated. He turns away and walks out through the opening he has come through and disappears.

I stare after him. I don't know what to do. The Jack I trusted, the Jack I was starting to care for, is gone.

Dominus gives a heavy sigh, breaking the tension. "I better go after him. Don't cry, Thea. He'll be all right. It will be all right."

He drops his beautiful head briefly against my chest and I hug it. I hadn't realized I was crying until he said so. Tears are leaving dirty trails down my face.

"Will, you can lead Iron and Thea out, can't you?"

The Mudgluck nods, looking upset, but Dominus goes on. "Thisss will work out jussst fine. Will isss the bessst one to help you now. Good luck, my friendsss."

He winks one of his emerald eyes at me, playfully flicks his tongue at Ironsides who glares at him grimly. Turning his enormous body he follows Jack's trail out of the opening and vanishes.

Will pats my knee. "They'll be fine, Thea," he says reassuringly.

Iron says nothing. He is lost in thought.

I sniff, wiping my face. I must look a mess, but I don't care. I take a deep breath.

"Ok, Will," I say, trying to sound tough and uncaring. "Which way out of this place?"

We travel all day with no incidents and by the time night is falling, we have reached the stairway leading to Stoneham. Unlike the stairs that led us down here, it doesn't go straight up, but weaves back and forth, a spiral into the sky. I am giddy looking up at it.

Will is sitting nearby, out of breath. His face is worried. I go over to him and drop to my knees to embrace him.

"Thank you, Will, I say gladly. "I'm happy it was you to lead me here. It is fitting, considering you were the first person I met here —" I stop speaking because Will is about to cry.

"Can't I go with you, Thea?" he asks plaintively. He sounds younger than ever.

Before I can answer, Iron grins at him.

"You're a good soldier, Waters," he says with his old roughness. "You've been the best of guides, but now we need you to go and let Broon and Ember —" he pauses here and glances at me, "and Jack and Dominus — know we've made it and we're all right."

Will's face is brighter.

"That would be great, Will," I assure him. "Be our messenger."

Will snaps to attention and gives me a small bow.

"Anything for the Queen of Thornwold."

I gape. Queen? Oh no.

"I was just getting used to Princess," I say ruefully.

"If all goes according to plan," Iron says, "you are the new Queen."

I laugh and hold up my hand. "Stop, stop! One uncomfortable title at a time, please."

Will laughs too and gets up, shouldering his small pack. "Okay, I'm off. Anything else I can do?"

I shake my head. "Thank you, Will. We'll see you at the end of this."

He grins at me, bows again, and waves to Iron. With a poof of dust, he dives into the path and is gone. My smile fades.

"Do you think he'll be all right?" I ask Iron anxiously.

"Oh yes, Mudglucks can travel fast as lightning underground. He and his family hollowed out many of the paths in this chasm, you know. He's safer on his own than he is with us."

We rest, drinking some water and eating some bits of food. I gaze up at the stairs again. I am hesitant to start the climb, knowing how long it's going to take, and how tired I am going to be by the time we reach the top. I am also loathed to spend one more night in the chasm.

"I think it's better to climb as far as we can in the dark. Less attention attracted this way. Not that it matters. I'm sure Malius knows we are coming so no surprise there."

"I wouldn't be so sure. Hopefully, he thinks we are still sitting in our, what did he call it? Tomb."

I shudder. We begin the climb. It's dark, but this staircase, unlike the other, has short sides to it making it less treacherous.

The higher we get, the clearer and lighter the air becomes. It makes sense as we are nearing the surface and walking against the setting sun. I stop and breathe in deeply.

"I never want to go back into that chasm," I pant. "My first order as Queen will be to fill it in."

Iron is holding on to my shoulder tightly. His claws scratch my neck.

"Shhh," he cautions. "I think I hear something."

I shrink back against the side of the staircase and blink into the darkness. We are extremely high now, hundreds of feet in the air. I'm warm from exertion, but there's a breeze blowing and its chilly. I wrap my cloak around me tighter and listen.

Ironsides is right. There's a faint far off swoosh of air stirring high above us. Terrified, I remember the dragon and fight my urge to look up. *Faces show up in the dark* says Jack's voice in my head. But this noise doesn't sound like a monstrous animal. It is a small whirl of wind, bouncing lightly off the cliffs above us.

We listen and a long low whistling sound comes on the breeze. It reminds me of something. I think inexplicably of the small flute in my pack.

"Iron!" I hiss. "The whistling in the woods! Back in Brell!"

I am excited. The whistling is significant. It has to be. This is the second time I've heard it. It has to be connected to me.

"It's Malius," answers Iron, low in my ear. "It must be."

My excitement fades. Is it Malius? But how? Is he flying? The whistle comes again, but farther off, well above us. It sounds different than it did in the forest. It isn't as beckoning as it felt before. Instead, it feels like a warning of some kind. But a warning to us? Or to something lying in wait for us on the path ahead? We listen, but it doesn't come again.

"I don't like it," mutters Iron.

Nor do I, and I wait to move until I'm confident the whistle is gone. Soon, we are climbing again. With each curve we round, I expect something to leap at us. But nothing happens. We circle upwards and the way is clear.

"With luck," I say, trying to shake off my unease, "we'll reach the top in the dark and we can take a long rest."

Ironsides agrees, but his voice is worried. His eyes are reflecting the faint light of the sun. We've climbed so high we've nearly beat it, going backward in time, but the orange glow is setting fast. Rays of crimson touch the turtle's shell, making the faded gold on his back shine.

Stoneham's Loss

Ironsides and I have reached the top. We stumble forward off the stairs and it reminds me of stumbling off the bottom of the steps into the chasm. This time, I don't fall so much as throw myself down. Mercifully, there is soft grass, so the landing doesn't hurt. We are outside the walls of Stoneham and the sun has set.

Iron has tumbled off my shoulder and is panting in the grass. He nibbles blades of it.

"Are you all right?" I examine him anxiously.

"I may need a moment," he says around his mouthful.

I roll over and lay on my back, staring up the high walls above us. They are partially crumbled in spots. Now that we are close to it, I can tell the city around the castle is large and spread out. There is no sound from behind the walls.

The staircase has taken us to a flat grassy plateau that stretches from the foot of the walls to the edge of the chasm. On this side, instead of the edges of trees and crumbling earth and rock, there is a low stone wall, so you might walk a path along the edge of the vast gap and not fall in. We lay on the grass in plain view of the high towers above us, but I don't care. All I can do is gaze up at the sky and not move. Eventually I stagger to my feet, my muscles screaming, and pick up Iron, who gives a small indignant noise.

"Sorry," I murmur to him. "But we need to be out of sight."

There are a line of trees along the walls. Between these, I sink down, rummaging in my pack for refreshment. I am nearly out of Lilywell water. I take a small swallow and give some to Ironsides.

"We need to be careful with our provisions," I say, breaking off a lump of cheese and giving it to him. "At least for a bit longer."

I don't finish the obvious thought. If we die, there won't be any need for food. If we live, well, hopefully there will be plenty of water and food in our future.

I take out the small map of Stoneham Broon had tucked into my pack in Lilywell. I spread it out on my knees, but it's too dark and I dare not conjure any light.

"Let's try and sleep for the night, Iron. When it gets light out, we'll find the way in."

Iron agrees and he is soon tucked away, small snores emitting from his shell. I am glad he is there, but for the first time since I started this adventure, I am terribly lonely.

Each hour brings me closer to facing Malius again. He won't let me break in and just smash the Globe. No matter what anyone thinks, Malius is no fool. I am convinced he knows exactly what I am after. He isn't going to let me have it. I am going to have to figure out a way to get to it and break it before he kills me.

I experiment a bit and watch the white glowing net of protection weave itself out of my hands and wrists. It's different now. Clearer. I don't even have to concentrate as much as I normally do.

I think of my life in Brell. Maggie's face and Thomas's laugh. Abigail's eyes when she smiles at me. Bol's kindness. I think of everything that has happened to me since I entered the forest and all the strange and wonderful characters I have met. I think about the glowing waterfall of lava in Ember's caverns, and Broon's peaceful house, and the pale green and golden beauty of the Thorn.

I remember Jack's story of his mother's people and my own parents. I wish they had lived. Perhaps we would have moved from Brell. Perhaps I would be safe in the university at Moor, pursuing study and ignorant there was ever a place called Thornwold.

Safe. Ignorant. The words echo in my mind and make me uncomfortable. A small voice inside tells me I am not sorry I came here. I am glad to have met the people I have met. I am even glad my parents were King and Queen of a magical world. I'm only sorry I'll never have the chance to explore more of it.

I watch Iron's shell. I wonder how to save him, for save him I must. I decide once we are inside the castle, I'll find someplace to leave him where it's safe and out of the way. He'll object, but I can't help it. I won't have him die because of me.

Once the sun rises, I open my eyes. I don't know where I am. I am lying in the grass underneath a tall birch tree. Its silver leaves shimmer in a soft breeze. It's barely dawn. The sun is throwing its long rays across the top of the chasm. I shiver, gazing at the early morning cloud cover. Whatever happens, I'm not going back down there.

Iron's head is emerging. He winks one bright eye at me, yawning. "I am much better. Despite where we are, I slept well."

I grin. "I'm glad to hear it. Because we may have a long day ahead."

I pull out the map of Stoneham again and unroll it. I lay it on the grass so Iron can see. The way into the secret passage is clearly marked in silver. I find the staircase on the map and am pleased we aren't far from the location of the entrance.

"It's around this corner." Iron takes a deep breath of clear air. "Are you ready, Thea?"

My heart has started pounding and I am pale.

"It's nearly done," reassures Ironsides. "Find the Globe, destroy it, and get out. That's all we have to do."

I resist the urge to laugh hysterically at this simple and encouraging explanation. I examine the map again.

"But where is the Globe? That's the problem."

"Don't you know I used to live here? I think it was part of the reason Broon wanted me with you. I can help. I know where many of the main rooms are, and some of the not so main rooms."

So much for my plan of leaving him behind somewhere. I'll have to protect him as well as I can. We creep around the edge of the castle walls. Set low in the wall, is a small door. Down a set of steps and well hidden behind some clumps of bushes, it stands partly open.

I pause. "Are you sure that's the secret entrance? It doesn't look very secret. And it's open."

He sounds uneasy. "Yes, that's it. I don't like it being open but —" he motions with his head at the ground around it. Long grass grows around the edges of the door. It has clearly been open for a long time.

"It must not be used frequently. Or perhaps ever."

Iron's claws squeeze my shoulder reassuringly. "Take a deep breath, Thea, and be prepared to shoot some of that blue flame if you have to."

We are in a long, stone passageway. Heavy, wooden doors lined either side of it. All of these stand open in splintered silence. A torch is burning dimly in a low sconce on one of the walls. There are no guards or prisoners. The place is deserted.

I take the torch and shine it past the door nearest me. I make my way down the silent and cold corridor. This isn't how I had imagined the secret passageways of Stoneham to be. The word 'dungeon' didn't even sink in. For me, dungeons existed in books and not in life, but this is a dungeon.

It isn't pitch black. Some of the torches on the walls are burning, but most are out. The stone walls are wet with dripping moisture.

The chilling part is the lack of prisoners and the violence with which they have been removed. Some of the doors are torn from their hinges. Some have been hacked open with axes. Each cell is empty, but I don't know how recent the emptiness is.

"Iron," I whisper, "are there supposed to be prisoners here?"

This doesn't make sense. Malius is terrible. His dungeons should be overflowing with imprisoned people.

Iron gives the familiar turtle gesture I interpret as a shrug. "Perhaps it isn't used any longer."

His words muffle in the air. The atmosphere in this place is similar to the chasm, thick and heavy. There is a quality to it making me sleepy. Iron's voice sounds tired.

We wander down the long passage. The hall has a few openings leading off in other directions. I peer down one of these. Only a few yards ahead it curves into shadow. I examine the scroll. The silver lines move straight ahead. I follow them.

Abruptly, I come to a split in the passage. One way leads left, another right. Both are dark and silent. I listen to the quiet and consult the map. The silver marks point to the right.

I'm about to turn this way when there is a faint sound. A soft whistle. I freeze. The nerves in my skin are tingling. Ironsides and I exchange glances.

I hold my breath. The whistling sound comes again. It doesn't sound like it did in the forest. Or on the stairs. There is no feel of a breeze or shifting of shadows. The sound is long and soft and low. I can't help it. I am pulled toward it.

Iron shakes his head as if rousing himself. "No," he whispers. "Thea!"

At the same moment, a gust of cool air comes up the left-hand passage and on it comes the whistle again. It winds itself around me and disappears. I pause and look to my right. The passage marked on the map as the right way slopes forward and climbs upward around a corner. Down the left-hand passage, the whistle is more insistent. Iron shakes his head fearfully, but I ignore him. I follow it.

The passage goes on for some way. As we walk, the whistle comes echoing out of it, dancing around my ears, bouncing off the walls. I touch the wall and it is sticky. Pulling my hand away, the liquid buzzes on my fingers. Something stirs in my memory, but I can't think what. Before long, something is looming ahead of us. Coming close to it I realize I am looking at a cage.

The bars are made of silver and gleam in the soft light of the torch. There is a heap of something inside. I ignore Ironsides, who is digging his claws into my shoulder as if to hold me back. Creeping closer, I stare. The heap is a man.

He stirs and moves slowly, sitting up from a pile of rags. He smiles vaguely at me. He is skeletal. His arms and legs are thin, white sticks covered in a ragged, black material. His shock of black hair is streaked with silver, and his pale face is thin and ill-looking. His shadowed eyes are dark. They watch Iron and me with a strange cloudiness.

"I am dreaming," the man says. His voice is a rasp from disuse. He appears to be speaking to himself, but his eyes clear quickly.

"I have dreamed you before. Speak, Spirit-Child."

I have jumped at the sound of his voice. It is achingly familiar.

Underneath the filthy beard and vacant expression, underneath the rags and the stick limbs, I see him.

"Iron. Oh Iron, do you know who this is?"

Ironsides is staring at the man, too. His face is stunned. "My God. It can't be."

"But it is," I say. "Papa."

My Papa is sitting in front of me, trapped by the silver bars of a cage. It's impossible, but here he is. His clear eyes have clouded over again, and he stares at the ceiling, humming. At my voice, he stops humming and his eyes refocus on me.

"You must go," he says uneasily. "I'm not supposed to have visitors."

"Ironsides. Help me."

I dig through my pack. I don't know what I am looking for. A key? A saw to cut the bars? I have nothing, but yet I keep looking.

"What is your name?" Ironsides asks him.

My Papa gazes at the turtle in surprise. "A talking creature. I have not seen a talking turtle in –"

He trails off, thinking hard. His face is confused and fogged with pain, as if trying to think hurts him.

"I don't know my name anymore," he finally says, focusing on Ironsides, "if I ever did. There was another prisoner here for a while. He called me Loss."

He smiles sadly. "Because I had lost everything when I was brought here. Even my name."

Giving up digging through my things, I glare at the cage. It has no door, only bars. Can I slice through them with some magic? Focusing my concentration, I throw a small stream of blue at one of the bars. It hits the metal and fizzles out quickly.

"Magic doesn't work," my Papa, now a man called Loss, says. He studies my face with interest. "It's kind of you," he says politely. "But no use, I'm afraid."

Iron stamps his foot. "We are going to get you out of there," he snaps. His small body is trembling. I remember Broon's words: *I have foreseen a role for him to play.* But what can a turtle do to break open a cage?

I don't know what to do. I stare at my pack's contents, spread out now on the floor. Food, water, maps, clothes, my Mama's pouch. As my eyes fall on the pouch I gasp.

"Iron!" I say. "The story!"

Iron is confused. "What story?"

I am already unrolling the scroll. "This is the story of Orpheus and Eurydice —"

Loss is sitting up straight to listen. His eyes are clear.

"Orpheus could play the lyre better than anyone in the world. He was in love with a woman called Eurydice and when she died of fever, he went into Hell to rescue her. He struck a bargain with Death. If he could play music and lure her spirit back to earth, she'd be restored to life, but he couldn't look back at her while he was doing it. He had to trust she would hear him and follow. Of course, he couldn't help it. He worried she wasn't following and looked back, and so Death won and kept Eurydice."

I pull out the flute.

"But this is a magic flute. This can break the bars and lead you out."

I say this last triumphantly to Loss. He sits very still.

Iron shakes his head doubtfully. "I don't know Thea. The story isn't the same. How could your Mother know your Father would end up here? How could she give you the right tools you need to save him?"

"I don't know, Iron, but she did!"

I put the flute to my lips and blow softly. A strange clear note comes out of the instrument and echoes around the chamber before vanishing into the air.

From nowhere, the familiar long and low whistle blows through the room. This time it is more distinctly accompanied by a soft breeze. It ruffles my hair, winds around Loss's face, and even taps Iron's shell, sending him jumping on my shoulder.

I don't know what it is. I don't know what it means, but I blow another note. The whistling breeze comes back. It's teasing. It blows a sharp gust at me and my hair whips around my face. Loss grins at it as it whirls by his shoulders.

"I don't know what it is," he says, echoing my thoughts, "but it has been my companion from time to time in this lonely place. A nearly human presence."

It comes back, blowing itself under my fingers holding the flute, and I glance down. Some of the magical symbols on the flute are glowing gold. Next to each is a hole. I put my fingers to each of these and lift the flute and blow as hard as I can.

The blast of noise that comes out of the small instrument rings through the room. At the same time, the bars around Loss glow. He scurries back from them as they grow brighter and brighter.

The musical note has become a song. There is a voice in it, although I can't understand the words, and for a moment I swear it is my Mama's voice.

The light goes out and with it the bars fade slowly and disappear. I gaze down at the flute as it crumbles into ash. The whistling breeze is gone.

On my shoulder, Iron swallows. Without bars between us, the man called Loss is even more worn. His hair is rough and hangs into his eyes. His skin is pale, nearly translucent, with years of imprisonment and illness. He leans forward and examines me closely. His dark eyes stare into mine for a long moment. He draws in his breath sharply.

"Thea," he says. His face is clear. The prison is gone. I throw myself into his arms and nearly knock him down. For a long time we sit, crying and holding each other. Iron, who has been knocked sideways by our embrace, crawls up on my Papa's shoulder and nuzzles his thin cheek.

My Papa laughs at this. His laughter is broken and raw with years of neglect. "Old Ironsides. My old friend."

"Your Majesty," Iron's voice is shaking with emotion. "We thought you were dead."

"I was dead, perhaps," says Douglas Morgan, "I was lost." He turns to me. "I'm afraid I'm weak, Thea. I am going to need your help."

I stand up, giving him my arm, so he can pull himself to his feet. His eyes widen as he looks at me.

"I left you a child! Here you are a woman! How many years has it been?"

"At least seven. I am nearly seventeen."

"And so like your Mother."

Iron is impatient. "No time for all that now! Thea, we've got to get the King out of here. This changes everything!"

I turn to him, surprised. "What does it change? What do you mean?"

163

"The plan we had," explains Iron, "It was a plan for you. But now, don't you see? Perhaps it doesn't fall to you after all."

I stand there, holding my Papa's arm, the true King of Thornwold, and absorb this idea.

But my Papa goes still. "I'm a King?" he asks. "What's going on?"

I look at him in horror. A moment ago he was clear and lucid, but now he is now looking at me with the same clouded expression he had worn when trapped by the cage.

"You are King of Thornwold, your Majesty," Iron explains worriedly.

But Douglas Morgan is again the man called Loss. He smiles vaguely and says nothing. I can only hope its temporary. Perhaps, if we can get him to Lilywell, Broon can do something for him.

I glare at Ironsides. "Do you think he sounds well enough to lead an army or rule a country? But you are right about one thing. We need to get him out of here."

With this I tug on my Papa's arm and we head back in the direction we came, going slowly because he is weak and needs to rest frequently.

His memory drifts in and out. By the time we get to the open door, he has remembered me and is asking me questions about all that has happened while he has been imprisoned. He remembers Brell and our friends there. He remembers my mother and weeps. For him, its recent and new. He keeps looking at me in awe, as if wondering why I am not still a child.

I explain as well as I can. All about me coming to Thornwold and meeting Ember and Broon and our mission to steal or destroy the Globe. I leave some of it out. The part about the dragons fighting, and leaving Lilywell without the others, and running into Malius in the chasm.

For some reason, I don't want to tell my Papa about the real dangers I have been in. I tell myself it is because he is too fragile right now to hear it, but it is a lie. I am ashamed of my moment of weakness in the chasm. Not only that, but I am making up my mind about something. Something that involves a deception on my part and convincing a stubborn turtle on the other.

I am relieved when we slip through the opening and back into the light and air. Outside, the sun has risen in the sky. It can't be more than mid-morning. The light is wonderful after the dark. My Papa stumbles forward and nearly falls. I catch him, but he steadies himself.

"I'm not used to the light," he says. He shades his eyes, and I can tell it's hurting him.

"You must sit down," I insist, leading him over to the shadow of the castle wall. "You need to rest." He slips down to the ground.

Ironsides is gazing at my Papa with a worried expression on his face. The King is paler in the sunshine than inside the gloom of the dungeons. His black hair is streaked with gray and silver. He is impossibly thin and frail and old. He is not my tall, strong, gentle Papa any longer, but a man broken by years of captivity and ill-treatment.

But I am not a child, waiting on the doorstep for him to come back and take care of me. In a flash, the little girl is gone, and I am standing on the edge of a chasm in a magic world, while the forest in the distance is shadowy and beautiful, even from this far away. I have a job to do.

"Iron," I say slowly. "This isn't right."

The turtle sighs resignedly and purses up his mouth, ready to argue. I press on before he can say anything.

"I need you to take my Papa and lead him back to the Forest of Thornwold. To Lilywell if you can."

Iron is indignant. "I can't leave you, Thea. And what about him? He can barely walk. He barely knows who he is."

"But he's going to have to try. I'll give him the map and what's left of my food and water. He's got you to help him. Meanwhile, I'm going to go find the Globe and destroy it."

I say all this very fast, as if saying it quickly will make it better.

Iron opens his mouth to argue with me but closes it.

I'm winning and I know it, so I glare at him, daring him to try and stop me. "Listen to me Iron. Broon said you have a role to play. Don't you see it must be this? Lead the King. Save the King. This is your role. This will give you your life back."

Even as the words tumble forth, I know I am right. I knew about the flute. I know Iron will be a man again if he helps my Papa.

The turtle is gazing at me, but he still doesn't say a word. He is torn between our unfinished business, his loyalty to the royal family, and hope.

"I'll be fine, Iron," I insist. "My magic is the same as Malius's. It is a mirror of his. I can protect myself. I can face him if I need to. You must help me. Save my Papa."

With this I stop talking because I'm going to cry, and Iron finally nods his head and clears his throat.

"We have no way of getting word to the others anyway," he admits. "They are going to start their war with the fake you at the head of the army soon, and you must be inside when it happens."

"Once I do what I'm supposed to, I will come back and find you both." I promise him.

I know it is an empty promise, but I must say all the right things.

Iron frowns at the King, slumped against the wall. "How are we going to tell him?"

I have stood and went over to my Papa. He is so tired.

"Papa," I say picking up Iron from my shoulder and transferring the turtle to his. "Ironsides is going to stay with you. When you are up to it, you both must take the staircase into the chasm. You must get to Broon's. There is something in the castle I need. Something to end this."

"Broon?" he says in a puzzled voice. "It sounds familiar."

My heart sinks, but I linger for a few minutes, trying to get him to understand me. There is a part of me that hopes he'll forbid me to go. Ironsides watches us both sadly.

Because of memory loss, or perhaps because of weary resignation, my Papa doesn't argue with me the way a father should argue with his daughter. He looks at me with cloudy eyes.

"Malius is dangerous," he says vaguely. "You must be careful."

I smile through tears. With a flick of my wrist I send a streak of blue and silver flame bursting out over the edge of the chasm. It hits the top of a standing rock formation, exploding it into dust. The sound is enormous, but nothing stirs behind the castle walls. Even Iron's eyes widen in admiration.

I tuck the map of the chasm into the King's hand. I take out a small item wrapped in a yellowed handkerchief and press it into his other hand. He unwraps it, puzzled, and gazes at it. His face is confused, but slowly recognition slips in and he wipes away a tear.

The small, worn portrait of my Mama, the one Will Waters gave me on my first day here, lies in his hand.

"My Cecilia," my Papa says. The blue and gold swirls out of him and surrounds us both.

I reach out and pat Ironsides. "You better be a human when I next see you," I say, but Iron ignores me.

"The Great Hall is the largest room near the top of the steps out of the Dungeons, Thea," he cautions. "There is a smaller room next to it, where the King would often go for private council."

He has the map of Stoneham rolled out and is making smudges on it. "Here, and here. Check these rooms first. Malius may keep the Globe somewhere there. If not, well, when in doubt, head for the tallest tower. But don't leave yourself without an exit. Or a place to hide."

I look up, craning at the towers above. There are four. One is a bit higher than the others. It is graceful and slim with a silvery roof.

"Stay out of sight as much as possible," Iron is saying. "Don't take any unnecessary risks. Don't face Malius unless you have to. Understand?"

"Yes, Iron. I'll be careful."

I want to hug him, but he is too small. Instead I hug my Papa one last time, clinging to him fiercely. I wink at Ironsides.

"I'll see you soon," I say trying to sound brave, and I slip back inside the dark dungeons of Stoneham.

The Globe

Inside, the gloom is stifling again. I grab one of the burned-out torches from the sconces and light it with a small burst of reddish flame. I make my way down the hall, leaving the light of the doorway behind me. I haven't got far when there is a gust of wind and a loud scraping noise. Every low-burning torch on the wall goes out except mine.

Whirling, I watch the small stream of daylight vanish as the door behind me slams shut. I rush back to it, but there is no handle on this side of the door. It is sealed fast and from behind it there is no noise of Ironsides or my Papa. I step back, trapped now in pitch blackness only lit by the bright circle of my torch, and choke back a cry.

The wind had felt foul, not like my soft whistling breeze. Malius knows I am here. My heart is pounding in my ears. I turn back and creep past the empty cells. This time, the darkness is menacing. As my torch light shines on the ruined doorways and splintered doors, I stop and take a handful of deep breaths, trying to calm myself. If I panic, I will never make it out of this place.

Finally, I come to the split passageway, and this time I take the right-hand way as the map directs. I follow this way for a long time. At least in this passage, there are no more cells with ripped open doors. The floor is even and slopes upwards. This must be the way. It's still black as the darkest night, but the air is less heavy.

Something looms in front of my feet and I trip, dropping my torch. Before it goes out, I see I am falling onto cold, stone steps.

Catching myself on one palm, there is a shooting pain in my wrist. I fall to the side and twist quickly into a sitting position. I can't see anything. It is so dark it's as if my eyes are closed, even though I am blinking. I grope in the darkness for my torch but can't find it. My wrist aches, and I move it slightly, gasping as I experience another shooting streak of pain. I hope it isn't broken, but the pain is intense, and I fear the worst.

With my good hand, I search inside my pack until I find Ember's small vial of silver potion. Pulling it out, I am startled to observe it glowing softly in the darkness. I pour a few drops of this on my wrist, and the pain dulls slightly, but doesn't go away. It must be good for open wounds, but not breaks or sprains. I swear. I have to go on as best I can.

The bottle has another use. Holding it up, I squint around in the tiny glow it casts. My burned-out torch is a few feet from the steps. I get up painfully and retrieve it. I try and throw a small flame with my uninjured hand. It shoots out and catches the torch awkwardly, but at least it lights.

Putting my healing vial away, I tear away a strip of fabric from my skirt. Wrapping my hurt wrist as tightly as I can using my teeth and one hand, I finally hold up my torch and glance behind me at the wide stone steps curving upwards and out of sight. *Another spiral staircase.* I am exasperated. Is there no other design for a staircase? But a glance at the map shows me this stair leads to the upper floors.

The stairs are endless, but not as endless as the ones climbing out of the chasm. Several times, I wish I hadn't given all my water to my Papa and Iron. Unexpectedly, a large wooden door looms in front of me and I nearly run into it.. In relief I push the round handle, and it swings silent open.

I step out into a silent empty hall. Its vaulted, arched ceilings are carved with flowers and birds. Opposite me, are rows of tall stained-glass windows. Sunlight shines through them and creates an array of colors on the pale stone floors. To the left and right of me the hall stretches emptily.

The walls are set with blind arcades. Red velvet chairs line the hall sporadically, designed for guests to seat themselves to rest or engage in court gossip. Each is covered in a thick layer of dust. I realize everything is coated with a layer of dust, even the floor. I lean back against the closed door behind me.

There is an eerie silence to this place. Where are the people? The servants? Even the empty-shelled soldiers? More importantly, where is Malius?

I cross the hall and peer out of the glass. Below me stretches an empty garden. Overgrown and withered topiaries cut into the mishappen images of giant animals dot the landscape. Winding paths run between these in spiral patterns. The grass is brown and dry. Beyond the high walls, the silent city sits in ruins. Beyond that, an empty plain.

No, not empty. Far away, there is a line of silver. It shifts in the distance, a wave on an unbroken sea. It is my army.

I walk quickly through the dusty hall, my footsteps echoing as I make my way toward what Ironsides had smudged on the map as the Great Hall. Any moment, I expect Malius to pop out from the air, smiling at me evilly, but nothing happens. I find the Great Hall doors and enter.

The Hall is a large empty room with a dais at one end. Far above my head, vaulted ceilings are carved with the same birds and flowers as in the hall outside, but instead of stone, the beams are made of wood. A large fireplace, large enough to hold me and several others, stands halfway along the room. On the dais, are two thrones. One is larger, but both are simple and plain. On the backs of each, a large letter 'S' is carved and circled with flowers. It is the same 'S' that is on my necklace.

As if encouraging me in this line of thinking, my necklace buzzes on my skin. I pull it free of my dress. Perhaps it is only the light streaming in through the high windows, but the lavender glass 'S' appears to be glowing softly. I touch it and it buzzes on my fingers in a ticklish sort of way. Something about it makes me feel I am not entirely alone in this strange place. I walk to the thrones and run my finger along the smaller one. They are both covered in years of grime. I decide Malius must prefer to do his ruling from somewhere else in the castle.

Opposite the thrones is a small door. I go to this and push it open easily. Inside is a much smaller room. The walls are hung with faded tapestries depicting various nature scenes. I realize they are showing different images of Thornwold. The castle of Stoneham, the plains outside, the forest of Thornwold, and one showing a wide desert and a great sea of swirling foam and graceful ships.

In the center of the room is a large table and chairs. Some of these have been knocked over as if the sitter rose up hastily. On the table are important looking papers, unrolled, and held down at the curling edges with small weights. There is a silver letter opener laying on one of these. I pick it up absently. The papers are yellowed, and the edges frayed. I examine one or two of these, but they appear to be written in several languages. I can't read them. Like the thrones, everything here is coated in layers of dirt. Besides the table, papers, and chairs, the room is empty.

Nothing touched. Nothing disturbed for all these years. Where does Malius live? It doesn't make sense. He wanted Stoneham. He wanted to be King. He wanted the grandeur, the power, the servants. This castle is empty and neglected. No one feasts in the Great Hall. No one cleans, cooks, or gossips. No one plots intrigues or writes laws or seeks counsel in this little room.

Where are you? I whisper to empty air. Stoneham is enormous. I am very small. I pick up a chair and right it. I sit down in it and spread out the map of Stoneham on the table. With the silver letter opener I draw a thin scratch on the Great Hall and smaller room next to it. I gaze at the hundreds of rectangles and squares and round towers that are left. I put my head in my arms on the table and listen to the silence.

Far above Thea, Malius is pacing back and forth in his quiet, silver tower. He knows where she is, watching her as she wanders through his empty halls, but he doesn't much care at this moment. After all, the Globe is well hidden, and she is one young girl, alone and friendless, mostly powerless.

He pauses in his pacing, considering. One of his hands is still wrapped in gauze. It is the hand that was burned on her white net of protection. The burn startled him. It had been years since he was hurt physically by anything or anyone. He raises it in front of his face and unwraps it.

The skin is red and blistered but healing slowly. He could rub some salve on it, heal it with a few drops, even a few muttered words of magic, but he prefers the pain. To let his body suffer while he watches, absorbing the sting of the burn and bleeding and the sweat of the accompanying fever. He is fascinated by the sensation of it.

Years ago, he had enjoyed hurting others. He used to beat that silly snake of his and draw blood. He used to beat his servants when he first became ruler of Stoneham. One by one, until they died or fled.

He turned to the dungeons and the torture methods there. He even lured the old King of Thornwold back to the Thorn with a few well-placed imitative cries. He had enjoyed inflicting pain on the pathetic man. The last of his enemies. The last of the family that had displaced his own.

But as the years went on, and he gained more control over the land of Thornwold and its citizens, he had lost interest in the infliction of pain. He gradually forgot about most of the prisoners in his dungeons, even the ex-King. Now, thinking about him, he supposes the King was dead long ago. A skeleton left inside a magical cage.

Malius sank into a kind of aimlessness. He wandered his lands. His magical powers made him invisible at will. He crossed the sea, leaving Stoneham unattended, but guarded by his empty soldiers. An empty shell of a castle filled with empty suits of armor. Malius preferred emptiness.

One evening he wandered into Brell. He had been there before of course. It was here the displaced royal family hid. It was here the mother had died and he had lured the father away. It was here he first saw the small Princess of Thornwold. She watched magic drifting in the air no one else could see. No one but himself.

At first he was afraid. He rushed back to the Globe and made sure it was safe. He realized something must have gone wrong. When he took possession of the Globe, the child should have lost her power, but she did not.

He watched her. He lingered near the edges of the trees in the Thorn and saw her grow up. She had power, but didn't know what it was, that was clear.

He saw other things. She had no friends. She was smaller than the other children. They often bullied her, calling her names, and

172

throwing stones. He felt a quiver. In his own childhood was a faint memory of a stone and a filthy name. He hadn't thought of it in years. He shut it down quickly.

The girl read books by the river in the afternoons, and she spoke to herself out loud about what she thought. She had a small turtle she spoke to about her struggles at school. He found himself liking the sound of her prattle. He learned about her desire to go to someplace else, a different town, a larger school. He learned she was unhappy.

A spark of something grew in him. A new desire. She was an orphan. She knew no one as smart as she was. Those ignorant peasants she lived among couldn't truly appreciate her cleverness. Her abilities. Her eyes were his, and she was getting older, watching his dark shadows swoop at her window. He made them to let her know he was there. An introduction of sorts. He knew it was nearly time.

His attempt to take her had been foiled by the strange whistling breeze. Remembering this, he felt uneasy. It was no magic he knew. He couldn't see it. Only a long low whistling breeze stirring the trees into action. Foiling his plans. But at least she was here, in his lands. He followed her.

In the caverns she had learned the truth about herself. Began to use her magic and met his son. His son. He felt a twinge of anger. She had been in his son's arms the day he sent the dragon after them. His ordinary human son with his dead mother's eyes. He thought of the woman of Datura. He thought of her lifeless face. She had been soft and weak and dangerous. Clinging to and loving him. He had felt clean and purged once he had killed her. If only he had killed the boy too. But he hadn't and now Thea stood in the circle of his arms, her beautiful gold rimmed eyes wide.

Her refusal of his generous offer. He had shown her the world she might have. The world she could have with him if not for the silly, childhood plaything. That turtle. A talking turtle, no less. Her white net of protection flaming around them both. Her beautiful eyes glaring at him in hate and fear.

And now she sits in her father's old rooms. Listening to the quiet. Malius watches her in his dark round scrying glass. She has come to him to take Thornwold back. Sweet girl. Clever girl.

Stupid girl. She refuses to be his. She'll burn in the white fire of her own net perhaps. Perhaps he'll even burn with her. To wallow in the hurt.

Malius has a surge of intense rage and brings his burned hand down hard on the table in front of him. He winces with the pain of it and smiles. He lifts his hand and examines his burned fingers again. Fascinating.

Outside the walls of Stoneham, near where the door to the dungeons had slammed shut so viciously, Douglas Morgan leans his head against his hands and breathes heavily. He is so weak. His memory lapses are getting less frequent, but he isn't gaining much strength. The small turtle next to him is pacing back and forth.

"Your Majesty," he says worriedly, "You must not worry. You must rest as long as you can."

The man shakes his head. "Please don't call me that, Ironsides. I gave up the throne, remember?"

"Indeed," says the turtle sharply. "Not only did you abandon your people, but you wandered off and left your daughter to take on the burden for you. She shouldn't be in this mess."

The man is ashamed. "I didn't know. I was out of my mind with grief when I crossed back into the Thorn. I swear Cecilia was calling me, but once I got to her, it was him, imitating her voice."

Ironsides ignores him. "Not only that, but did you never think of what it might mean for me? To stay a dumb turtle in detestable Brell for the rest of my life? Which is sure to be long because you know –" He waves one of his clawed feet, indicating himself. "Turtles can live to be hundreds of years old."

This amuses the former King, who grins broadly. "Same old Iron." He carefully eases his thin frame to his feet, groaning. "We have to help Thea, Ironsides." He walks over to the door, which is sealed, and gives it a weak kick.

The turtle appears even more grim. "We can't do anything for her. We have to get to Broon's if we can. I don't see how though.

You can barely walk, let alone walk miles. I should have went with her. She'll never find the Globe by herself."

"My worry is she'll find Malius first."

"It shouldn't happen. Not if everything works out as it's supposed to."

"And when does anything work out the way it's supposed to?"

Ironsides pauses, looking at the King as if an idea has occurred to him. It is nearly mid-day. He cranes his head at the sky and paces back and forth.

"We can't make it to Lilywell on our own," he says, listing out their choices. "We can't get back inside the castle. But maybe we can make it to Broon. The plan should be in full swing now."

As if in answer, the two hear the faint far-off sound of marching feet. Hundreds climbing the chasm's spiral staircase. King Douglas of Thornwold stands up and turns to the sound. His eyes gleam.

Across the plains, Jack is riding grimly at the head of the army. They are nearly there. The ruined city surrounding the castle looms closer. He can see a line of Malius's soldiers lining the broken walls. Waiting. Next to him, shimmers the faint magical form of Thea. Her ghost grins at him and something sparks down inside himself, despite the fact he knows she is only an illusion.

He remembers their last interaction with a pang of shame. She had been right. He was jealous of her. Jealous of her fame and situation. He remembered the disappointment in her face and grimaced. He would make it up to her. Surely she would survive this. Surely they would win.

He gazes up at the far-off gleaming warm stones of Stoneham. A glint in the tallest tower catches his eye. Sun on glass perhaps. Or movement. A sparkle of water appears and falls from one of the windows in the tower. It glistens in the sun, dropping down and turning over in the air catching the light. Jack squints at it. Not water. Someone inside has broken the window.

Behind him, Broon and Ember stand on a distant hill. Together they watch the hundreds of Thornwoldians, peasants and soldiers alike, marching across the plains. Among them are the tribes of Datura, the Seafolk, and behind them come the magical Light Mountain people, their white robes gleaming in the sun.

Ember's beautiful face is troubled. "The Dark Monks," she says to Broon, but he shakes his head.

"Not yet," is all he says.

She can't tell if he is hopeful or not.

I lift my head. A faint noise has come from behind one of the tapestries in the wall, like the tinkle of glasses breaking in a pub far away. I stand up, gathering up the map and stuffing it into my pack. I step toward the tapestry and pull it. It comes away easily. There is an opening there. A set of winding stairs lead upwards and I stifle a groan. But this stair isn't on the map, and wherever it goes isn't on the map either. With a twinge of hope, I begin the climb.

Malius has heard the approaching blast of trumpets signaling an army. He strides to the window and glares down. Shrugging at the mass of people marching toward Stoneham, he watches his own empty-shelled soldiers move through the broken city. Where the front gates of the city should be, a heap of twisted metal sits. He hasn't bothered to repair the gates in years. No one has ever dared attack Stoneham. Or what is left of it.

Curious, he turns back to his dark glass and gazes into it to get a closer view of the army of people approaching him. His eyes widen. There, at the front, is his own son. Next to him, Thea, her red hair gleaming under the bright helm, her eyes laughing at the boy next to her. He knows it's an illusion, only a mere trick of a magic. She is downstairs slumped over her father's old scrolls. But it enrages him all the same. How dare she look at his son that way?

With a fierce movement, he throws the dark scrying glass through the window nearest him. It shatters it with a satisfying crash and Malius watches as the pieces fall hundreds of feet, glittering in the sun. He strides over to a shelf and rakes a handful of dark ash from a glass jar. With a movement like flame, he disappears into the air.

I reach the top of the stairs by sheer will only. I am so hot and thirsty I can hardly think straight. The staircase leads right into wooden trap door. I push against it. Locked.

I sit down on the steps and stare miserably at my pack. Of all the things to bring, I brought a change of clothes, food, water, a healing potion, and my Mama's pack, which now contains an old scroll and nothing else. I couldn't have thought to bring a hammer? A mallet to break down locked doors?

The dry sound of my laugh echoes around the small stairwell. I stand up and back down the steps a few paces. My wrapped wrist is still aching, so I aim my uninjured hand at the trapdoor.

The blast is so powerful the door disintegrates into dust. When the smoke clears, sunlight streams through the hole. I climb the stairs and find myself in a circular room. It's empty. Wind blows through a broken window. Shelves cover the walls. Books of all sizes and shapes line these, accompanied by curious objects in glass jars. Vials of glowing potions, bubbling liquids, and even one full of a tiny tornado of whirling air are tucked into corners. In the center of the room is a large chair and a small table. I step toward it curiously.

It is an ordinary, slightly worn armchair. One you might find in an old man's library or in the common room of a pub. Bol has several around the fire at Owl's Roost. Next to it is the table on which sits a small lamp.

I am puzzled by this room. It has none of the dusty grandeur of downstairs. Instead, it has a coziness to it. I could curl up in the chair with a book and soon be absorbed in its pages. This picture is such a direct contrast with an evil magician high in his magic tower brewing evil potions it makes me uneasy. If it weren't for the glass jars of magic, I could believe I was in my old schoolmaster's cottage in Brell.

I walk to one of the tall windows and gaze out. The lines of the armies moving toward Stoneham are still far away but getting larger. Clouds surround them. A glint of something flashes on a distant hill.

I turn away, my anxiety growing. Jack is down there somewhere. Broon. A shimmering magic me designed to trick Malius. I glance around the tower room. The army is too far away for Malius to see me there, but I don't think he would be fooled by a magical image of me.

I remember the blast of foul wind sweeping through the dungeons and locking me in. Malius knows I'm here. I'm certain of it. And since this plan of a distraction isn't going to work, and I am here and don't know where the Globe is, I may as well ask him. He might be in this room now, invisible, watching me.

"Where are you?" I say conversationally to the room. "Come out."

There's no answer.

Not here then. I draw my breathe and concentrate, sending a Seeking spell around the room. It hums busily here and there and taps the walls experimentally. It spends time in an empty space on top of a high bookshelf, but finally it swoops toward the floor, disappearing through the trapdoor. I try to call it back, but it is gone.

Hoping I haven't made a mistake, I am about to leave and descend the twisting stairs, when there is a scream like the scream I heard in the forest of Thornwold. The floor shakes and all the glass jars rattle dangerously on their shelves.

An immense black dragon rockets past the tower, its massive tail swinging behind it, narrowly missing the roof above me. It screams and draws its smoking breath in deep as it goes firing toward the front lines of the army. Not just front lines. People and creatures I care for.

I open my mouth to cry out, but there is a light rising from the hill behind the enormous army. The place where I saw the flash of light glows green and gold and spreads outward. It rises into the air like an enormous bubble. As it grows, it covers the army and reaches toward the beast in the sky. The dragon slows itself in the air, but its effort to stop is in vain and the bubble touches it. Immediately, both dragon and bubble dissolve into nothing.

There is no pouring of ash from the sky as there was in the field on Broon's lands. The bubble doesn't blow up with a bang, knocking anyone over. It is simply gone, taking the beast with it. The army marches on, unperturbed.

It must be Broon on the hill, and Ember, and hopefully those Light and Dark Monks they keep talking about. If their combined powers can defeat the biggest fire-breathing dragon I've ever seen, we might win this thing. I have to find the Globe.

I turn toward the staircase again with a renewed sense of purpose and stop. Malius is sitting in the worn armchair, watching me.

"Good Afternoon, Thea," he says lazily and smiles at me. I wish he hadn't. His smile is measured, watchful, and icy. The sight of him makes me cold all over.

"Hello Malius." To my relief, I don't sound scared. I think quickly. "Too bad about your dragon."

Malius laughs. It's a hair-raising sound.

Long ago in Brell, I saw a madman sent to the lunatic asylum in Moor. He leaned from his seat in the wagon as far as the chains would allow him and beckoned the people to come closer, which no one did. His eyes were bloodshot and staring. His laughter had no joy in it.

Remembering this, I try to hide a shudder. I turn away from Malius slightly, as if I am looking out the window again, but I keep him in my peripheral vision and think hard.

I could blast him out of the way and make a run for the stairs, but I believe he'd be after me in a moment, and the staircase is narrow. I could throw the net of protection around myself. We've already established it burns him, but could I keep it around me and move quickly at the same time? I doubted it. I didn't like being so close to the window. If he hit me with a blast, I could easily go through it.

But he isn't moving at all. When I look at him again, he's watching me curiously, as if waiting for me to speak. He doesn't appear agitated or ready to fight.

"Are you sending your empty-shelled men to fight?" I ask him neutrally.

He puts his head on one side. "I imagine they'll be leaving the gates shortly. They put themselves back together you know. Even the ones in the rubble of the chasm if they've at last made it out of the rocks. Even the ones pulled apart by the Thorn. They are all coming. So it will soon be over."

He says this in a bored way, as if he can't be bothered with the fact two armies will tear each other to pieces in front of his precious Stoneham. I'm abruptly angry with him and my anger pushes my fear aside.

"What is it all for?" I ask him sternly, lecturing a naughty child, "This castle? That ruined city? You don't even care about the people who live in this land. You don't have any riches. This, its empty and disused. What's the point?"

I glare at him gesturing around at the castle walls and the scene below us. His face is blank. I think I've startled him, perhaps angered him, but he puts his head on his hand and smiles at me again.

"It's often something I've wondered myself, *my* Thea," he says.

The way he says my name, with emphasis on the 'my' makes my skin crawl. He stands up and takes a step closer to me, his oddly handsome face looking down at me.

"How perfect you are for me," he says softly.

This is not what I had expected at all. I instinctively take a step back, touching the windowsill behind me, the cool wind blowing through the smashed glass.

He moves closer. His tone is eager, "I knew you were my match almost as soon as I saw you. A child, with magical ability to mirror my own. You are perfect. As you grew, you were not only beautiful, but smart. I had to have you. I nearly did once, but your father called for you, and you ran away from me, back into your cursed village."

I am horrified. He leans in and touches my face gently. I pull away from him, expecting him to get angry, but he only laughs.

"I waited until you were grown. Your mother died. That was convenient. Your father, I got out of the way."

My brain is scrambling to make sense of his words. The color swelling from him is the odd mix of black and bright green I had seen before. I shrink back and before I can stop myself, flick it away with my good wrist.

180

Malius's face darkens. He slaps me. Hard. I have never been struck in my life. I am knocked to the floor, blinded by the blow, my ears ringing. I raise my head slowly as he towers over me.

I blast him. He sees it coming a split second too late. I send angry blue fire into his chest and the force throws him against the bookshelves with a crash. Glass vials of smoking potions and glowing objects rain around him. He lays still and I am up and running for the trapdoor, hoping he is knocked out.

Magic, deep red and silver in color, lifts me from my feet and flings me backward toward the windows. I tense myself to strike them and go through, but he stops my body in midair and throws me to the floor. Laying still, I groan softly. If my wrist wasn't broken before, it is now.

He is standing over me. "You are challenging, Thea. That's what I enjoy about you. Your spunk. Your fire. But you are no match for me. I will be your teacher. I'll teach you everything you need to know."

I sit up slowly, carefully. I don't want to risk another attack. I decide to play along.

"I didn't know you were so brilliant." I can't keep the shaking out of my voice, but I hope he thinks its awe and not terror. "I was told so many lies about you."

Malius appears to believe me. He walks over to his chair and sits down, casually examining a rip in his sleeve where the bookshelf tore it.

"They all tell lies about me," he agrees. "I'm sure the lot of them think I'm a monster. They aren't completely wrong. I am a monster of sorts."

"But you are misunderstood," I say, thinking fast. If I can get him to believe I'm sympathizing with him, even willing to be in love with him, then maybe I can get him to tell me where the Globe is.

"Yes," agrees Malius sadly. "Misunderstood."

He is sidling nearer me again. This time, instead of a caress, his hand grips my arm with an iron strength. He pulls me close to him and begins to speak urgently in a low voice.

"When I left home to retake Stoneham, my family laughed at me. Laughed! I showed them all. I stole the Globe and hunted them down and had them imprisoned in my dungeons. Even my

181

father and mother. Especially my mother. She told me daily how I would never amount to anything. I enjoyed torturing her most of all."

The memory of the line of shattered doors and broken hinges, along with the emptiness and the darkness and the chill of the dungeons below makes me gape at him in horror.

"Come and see it," he says low into my ear, "Come and see these liars."

He turns me to face the window and we look down at the battle below. Dimly visible through clouds of dust, thousands of figures are fighting desperately on the plains outside the city walls.

Even as Malius's silent soldiers march out of Stoneham and drive the Thornwoldians back, I can see the dim outline of Broon and Ember. They are small glowing figures on the faraway hillside, their hands raised, the air flying thick with magic. Clouds of Quickwillow are descending on the black shells of armor. They rise and fall in a shimmering haze.

I see Jack, his hair matted with blood and dirt. His whole body stretched taunt and blazing with fury as he swings his sword this way and that. His face is set in grim lines. Pausing, he looks up and it's as if he is looking straight at me. He grins wildly, Serafin's sword flashing as it cleaves a magical soldier's head from his hollow shoulders.

But no, something is wrong. Jack flounders in the sea of bright swords. Two, no, three, empty-shelled men are on him, and he is gone – gone – under the feet of thousands.

Malius turns me to face him. His blue and gold eyes are utterly lacking in human sympathy

"Too bad about my son."

I spit in his face. In a rage, he is on top of me, his hands around my throat. His handsome face distorted with fury.

"He won't have you," he whispers. "And you won't find it. You will never find it. It is mine."

I can't breathe. I am choking, my vision is going blurry. My hearing is fading. I close my eyes. I can't think. I try to build a protective net, but nothing is happening.

Inside my head, there is a soft whistle. A softer breeze ruffles my hair. But no, it isn't inside my head. The whistle is in the room. Malius is gone, crawling away from me in terror. I am breathing again, in slow gasps that hurt. My throat is bruised, but my vision clears.

The breeze rustles around me for an instant, concerned, and then with an ear-splitting whistle it goes inside my chest. No, not inside me, but into the gleaming, golden necklace. Inside the lavender glass 'S', it burns and sings.

As before, when releasing my Papa from the magical bars, the noise of the song grows louder and louder. Sitting up, I realize not only it is coming from the glowing glass in the 'S', but something in the room is singing back to it.

Among the bookshelves, high on the tallest shelf, is a blank space. The singing is coming from here, but I don't know how. With one eye on Malius, who is sitting in the farthest corner of the room, his hands over his ears, his eyes shut tight, I get slowly to my feet.

I hold up my good hand and send a blast of white magic toward the space. Even as Malius leaps and screams toward me, the white net hits the empty space, tears something loose from the darkness, and then bounces away, surrounding him.

It burns him. He claws at it and I get out of the way, dropping my hand, willing it to disappear, but the net has taken on a life of its own and it clings to him. His face is red and blistered. His hair is smoking. He struggles toward the window, and in an instant I realize what he is going to do. But I don't move to stop him. I stand there, watching him as he throws himself through the shattered window and disappears. The wind is sweeping its way through the room, clearing the air of the smell of sizzling flesh.

I collapse. My knees give way as the singing stops. The wind leaves the necklace and with it all my power goes. Without it, I can't stand.

I gaze at the floor beneath the shelf that had held the Globe, which had been secreted in an invisible chamber. Malius had been right. I never would have found it. The remains of it lay in shattered pieces, black and smoking bits of purplish glass. My necklace is warm. I lift it up with my good hand. Matching black and smoking glass, once lavender, shines in the 'S'. It vanishes, leaving only golden flowers carved around its empty space.

ENDINGS

The walls are shaking. I have to get up, but I can't move. My wrist is useless, my throat is aching, my head is whirling with the loss of my magic.

I lay on the floor in the tower room and books and potions crash around me. From far away, my name is called.

Thea!

I manage to raise my head and peer through the smoke and haze the broken vials of magic are making. I try and shout back, but my voice is hurt, damaged, and comes out in a hoarse whisper.

A dim figure bursts through the trapdoor. In a moment there is a man beside me. I don't recognize him, but I have seen him before. In a dream perhaps. His hair is gray, his face is lined, his beautiful eyes are bright and sardonic.

'Thea, my child," he is saying. He lifts me in surprisingly strong arms. "You must hold on," he says. "Let me carry you as you've carried me so many times."

I nod my head because I can't speak. His words don't make any sense to me. The man looks towards the wall as it collapses inwards. He dives for the trapdoor, carrying me with him. He staggers down a set of circular stairs as it crumbles beneath us, half-running, half-falling toward the door of the small room next to the Great Hall.

As the walls around us fall away, high snow-covered mountains rise behind us stretching into the distance. On the air comes the light scent of the sea.

Later, Ironsides tells me the whole story. He sits beside my bed in the small room in Stoneham they have spruced up for me. It is clean now, and there are servants bustling in every direction. It isn't at all the empty, eerie, dirty castle I had wandered through days earlier.

After I had left them at the door to the dungeon, they had sat outside it and my Papa had rested there for a long time. As the sun climbed higher, Iron had worried. He debated trying to get my Papa down the winding staircase and through the chasm, but he knew it wouldn't work. The King was too weak.

While they were debating, they heard the noise of marching feet coming up the staircase behind them. Thinking it was Malius's soldiers, they started to hide behind the thin trees near the castle walls. But it wasn't Malius's soldiers. Instead, the hoods of hundreds of Dark Monks appeared, marching up the stairs on their way to join the armies on the plains.

My Papa called out to Monk Wulfsiege, who is the leader of the Dark Monks, and recognized the King. He also recognized Ironsides and thinking the turtle had rescued the King single-handedly from the dungeons in an attempt to restore him to the throne, he immediately broke the enchantment set on the turtle years ago.

Of course, eventually the whole story came out, but Monk Wulfsiege was even more impressed at Ironsides' role in helping me all the way from Brell to Stoneham, and the unswerving loyalty to my family all these years. He even joked that the vows of silence Iron would have taken as a monk were already done, as he had had to live in Brell for nearly twenty years and was unable to utter a single word in all that time.

Iron and my Papa were taken to Broon and Ember, who were responsible for the flash of silver on the hill I had seen from the tower. Together with the Dark Monks, they created the brilliant bubble destroying the massive ash dragon.

They rode into battle, and when some of the older Thornwoldian soldiers saw my Papa, they recognized the King at once. The word spread that not only had the King returned, but he had defeated the dragon as well. This rallied the armies of Thornwold, and they fought hard and fiercely. In spite of this, they were beaten back again and again, until I destroyed the Globe.

The empty-shelled soldiers had simply fallen to lifeless pieces, and the war ended. It must have taken a while for the tower built by Malius to fall, because it took Iron some time to cross the battlefield and get into the castle, but he found me in time.

I am happy for my turtle, but I miss his small green shell and grumpy face. Iron, as he still prefers to be called, sits by my bedside a lot these days.

Ember, her eyes happier than I remember them, sits beside him as much as she can, when she isn't being called away to nurse the wounded. The Great Hall has been turned into a hospital of sorts for the armies, and Ember is kept busy day and night tending to patients with her silver phial.

Most have come through the battle, though not unscathed. Dominus has a new wound on his neck. It will leave yet another scar. Will Waters has lost part of an ear, but since he is a Mudgluck, he will be able to grow another.

Jack was terribly injured. When he was trampled before my eyes, he had barely survived. For days he hovered between life and death, the gaping wound to his head festering and seeping. On the third day, I pulled myself into his room and ordered him to get better.

When he didn't open his eyes, I leaned in and kissed him firmly on the mouth. Exhausted, I fell asleep in the chair next to his bed. When I woke, he was awake, smiling at me weakly. I wasn't Prince Charming, and he wasn't Sleeping Beauty, but he did recover after that, so perhaps there's more power in a kiss than anyone knows.

Speaking of exhaustion, it's all I can do to drag myself out of bed these days and around the room. My Papa says it will get better and easier with time but getting used to losing one's magical ability is a struggle.

It changes the way you move and breathe. I can't get used to how funny my vision is now I don't see colors coming off of people, or rather, I don't see magic any longer. My eyes have changed to an ordinary blue with ordinary pupils. The gold bits are gone forever.

I told Broon I don't mind. Each time I look into a mirror, I would have seen Malius's eyes gazing back at me, and it would have reminded me of the tower and things I'd rather forget.

Broon smiles at me gently. He says it is better this way. He went to sort through the debris left by the tower and found Malius's body himself. He took it away and buried it someplace deep in the Thorn. He looked for the remains of the shattered glass Globe, but they had disappeared.

I told he and my Papa about the whistling wind, and how it had saved me. Broon said it was curious the same piece of glass that had made the magical Globe had been used to make my Mama's necklace.

He knew nothing of it, and he couldn't imagine how it was done. As for what the strange, whistling wind might have been, he only pats my shoulder with his strong brown hand and leaves my Papa and I to wonder.

Months have passed. My Papa has been restored to the throne. I am glad of this, as I had no desire to be the Queen. I don't even have much desire to be the Princess, to be honest.

My Papa's memory was fully restored in time. Sometimes, he is dreamy, but he has lost the blank, cloudy look that would come and go. It's a good thing too, because ruling a country is hard work. Especially coming out of an economic downturn and shaking off a repressive regime.

Now I am recovered, I spend a lot of time with Jack, and a lot of time reading up on Thornwold's magical history. The library at Stoneham is enormous.

Sometimes I have a pang of homesickness for Brell, and for Abigail, our cottage by the river, and Maggie and Bol and Thomas. Papa is the only one who understands. He misses an ordinary life too. Sometimes he says what he wouldn't give for a pint from the Owl's Roost and good chat with Bol.

It will be autumn soon, and the cool winds are sweeping across the plains here in the evenings. Autumn reminds me of the cozy fire in Owl's Roost, and the clink of cutlery in the Great Hall reminds of the clink of glasses in Bol's pub.

Lately there have been whispers among the Watchers in the Thorn. Broon is troubled and weary when he visits the King. I listened at the door of my Papa's study but couldn't hear a thing except the word 'Brell' and something about the forest rivers drying up and the mists getting thicker. I worry over this, but Jack says to leave it, and we'll travel to the Thorn soon to find out for ourselves.

I can't help but think of Malius's body, slowing rotting in the ground. If the rivers are shrinking and the trees are dying, I wonder if it is because there is some poison seeping from his remains to the roots of the Thorn. Sometimes I dream he is standing in front of me, his blue and golden eyes watching me with reproach and regret and hunger. Then he looks beyond me at something I can't see.

I want to know what it is: colors of magic or Stoneham's warm walls. Or the green and golden silence of the trees, the stillness of Broon's lily pools, or the shimmering motes of magic fallout over a lava lake.

The End

About the Author

Hollan L. McCarthy has degrees in liberal studies, education, and is working on another in library science. She lives with her husband and their cat in Washington state.
This is her first novel.

Made in the USA
Middletown, DE
24 October 2020